In The Shadow Of The

Mammoth

Patricia Nikolina Clark

Illustrations by Anthony Alex LeTourneau

Step into the Ice Age with me!

Patricia Nikolina Clark

Blue Marlin Publications

"This is a story certain to captivate young and adult readers alike. Zol's story has universal appeal as the rite of passage of a young man bounded by tradition and driven by destiny. With a storyline certain to stimulate the imagination of all who share even a remote interest in the lore of ancient times, the action is quick-paced and written in a straightforward, lively prose. The ending will certainly leave the reader wanting more, and we can all hope that Patricia Clark will not let this gem of a tale end here."

—Jerry R. Galm, Ph.D.
Professor of Anthropology
Eastern Washington University

"Patricia Clark definitely did her homework regarding the archaeology of the Clovis culture, and she has turned what little we do know into a fantastic story full of emotion, humor, and suspense. This is a must read."

—Powys Gadd
Forest Archaeologist / Heritage Program Manager
Okanogan and Wenatchee National Forests

"I found this book very interesting and quite fascinating to read."

—Rosalie Baker
Editor, *Dig* and *Calliope* Magazines

"Patricia Clark has provided us with a creative and insightful look into the world of the Clovis People. She provides the reader with wonderful details and descriptions of the world in which they lived; a world of ice and cold winds, with forests, grassy steppes or plains containing huge creatures like mammoths, mastodons, giant ground sloths and gigantic bison—all now extinct. It is a world that begs us to use our imagination and dream of the trials of ice age life for the scattered bands of people who lived—and died—during that difficult time.

"This is an exciting tale of one boy's self-discovery and dangerous journey into adulthood. And while this journey is set in the Ice Age, the lessons this boy learns are appropriate for our own sons and daughters today."

—Dr. Keith Williams
Director
Wenatchee Valley Museum and Cultural Center

"Ms. Clark skillfully presents information regarding tools, hunting techniques, shelter, food and clothing, and many other aspects of the prehistoric world while maintaining a page turning plot line. Readers will thrill to the excitement of Zol hanging from a cliff edge over a raging river and feel shivers down the back as the trunk of a woolly mammoth touches him. This novel provides a refreshing twist to the traditional historical fiction genre. It is one that I would strongly recommend to any intermediate school aged student—a captivating read!"

—Ms. Karen Kneadler
Librarian
Seoul International School

In The Shadow Of The

Mammoth

Patricia Nikolina Clark

Illustrations by Anthony Alex LeTourneau

Foreword by Richard Michael Gramly, Ph.D.

A Blue Marlin Publications Paperback

Blue Marlin Publications
823 Aberdeen Road
West Bay Shore, NY 11706
www.bluemarlinpubs.com

Text copyright © 2003 by Patricia Nikolina Clark
Illustrations copyright © 2003 by Anthony Alex LeTourneau
Book design by Jude Rich
Cover design by Anthony Alex LeTourneau and Jude Rich

First Edition: June 2003

Printed and bound by Friesens Book Division in Altona, Manitoba, Canada

Clark, Patricia
    In The Shadow Of The Mammoth / by Patricia Nikolina Clark; illustrated by
Anthony Alex LeTourneau. —First Edition
        p.   cm.
    Summary: Zol, a Clovis boy, must face his fears and join the Star Dancers in
the hunt for the Wooly Mammoth.
Library of Congress Control Number: 2003104288
    ISBN: 0-9674602-4-7
    CIP information available.

Acknowledgements

I am deeply grateful to R. Michael Gramly, Ph.D., who in 1990 allowed me to tag along during an excavation of Clovis artifacts at the Richly Clovis Site in East Wenatchee, WA, and patiently answered all my questions. His zest for bringing the Ice Age alive to the school children who visited the dig daily fueled my imagination and kept me going when my own enthusiasm faltered.

I am indebted to many others: To Keith Williams, Ph.D. (Director) and Mark Behler (Curator) at the Wenatchee Valley Museum and Cultural Center, Wenatchee WA, for giving me free access to the Clovis research materials in the museum archives and for lending me support whenever I asked. To Andrea Parker, who shared with me her experiences of raising crows as a child, and to Liz and Mike Eggers, who allowed me to visit their pet crow, "Lucky." Because of them, "Koot" became a real character in the story.

To Dan Stephens, Ph.D., Ornithologist, and Warren Scott, Geologist, both of whom read early drafts and gave helpful comments. To Peg Kehret and Bruce Coville, who encouraged me to pursue publication and who mentored me with advice—and by example, through their own writings. To Meghan Nuttall Sayres, for all the times she dropped her own writings and listened to me when I needed it.

Finally, and most gratefully, to Bruce Foxworthy and the Wenatchee Valley Writers Group, without whose loving encouragement and critical support I could not have completed this project.

Thank you all!

To Bruce Foxworthy, for planting the seed,
and to the Wenatchee Writers Group,
for nurturing its growth.

Author's Note

Approximately twelve thousand years ago, a group of nomads known as the Clovis People roamed North America hunting woolly mammoths with stone-tipped spears.

Archaeologists know this from artifacts found in excavations all across the continent. But there is no written history from that time, so scientists can only guess how they lived.

Perhaps the Clovis hunters watched and learned from the wolves how to work together as a "pack" to bring down an animal much larger than they were.

Living in small groups of about twenty people, the Clovis would be smart to follow the wolves' example. One mammoth could provide food for months, as well as hide for shelter and bone for tools.

This is the story of Zol, a Clovis boy. He lived at a time when beavers were as big as bears. When the scream of a sabre-toothed tiger could still pierce the night. When a moving mountain of hair could suddenly block out the sun.

This was the time of mammoths.

This was the Ice Age.

FOREWORD

By Richard Michael Gramly, Ph.D.
American Society for Amateur Archaeology

Archaeological excavations in 1988 and 1990 of the East Wenatchee Paleo-American site in central Washington State and its spectacular cache of ancient flaked stone artifacts were closely reported in Newspapers, on Television, and in scientific journals. More than 11,000 visitors trekked to the site in order to observe a tool kit that had been stored within a pit by hunters, who for unknown reasons, never reclaimed their still-useful property. Among more than 55 artifacts left behind were Clovis fluted spear points and 14 enigmatic bi-beveled rods of proboscidean (mammoth or mastodont) limb bone. Two of these rods bore rarely seen designs common to Ice Age peoples of Europe and Asia. The finds at East Wenatchee inspired a score of artists – including painters, photographers, graphic designers, and writers. Among them was author, Patricia Clark.

Patricia's entertaining and highly plausible story amplifies and builds upon the restricted insights furnished by scientific archaeology. One may believe that children who long ago inhabited the Columbia River valley near East Wenatchee played just like Zol, Keena, and Tungo did and, too, had to cope with perils – both real and imagined. From our perspective of 12,000 years, we admire hunters who walked in the shadow of the mammoths when the New World was first peopled. Theirs was a special privilege given to few human beings. The chance to set foot on new lands will come again only when explorers leave Earth for other planets and the stars.

The story of Zol's band of Clovis hunters has the ring of truth. Patricia Clark's informed speculation about the past is respectful, and it is refreshing to behold an author who so dearly loves her native land and the creatures who once inhabited it. Her perspective is as relevant to the present day as it is to the bygone Ice Age. I can only hope that some future chronicler will care to treat our own culture of the 21st Century in such a gentle and understanding manner. Let this future writer be assured that Koot and his kind still thrive!

Contents

That Dream!	1
Father, I'm Back	6
Mammoth Camp	11
A Baby Crow	14
What Good Is A Crow?	18
The Spear-thrower	21
Wolf Dreams	27
Sacred Mammoth	32
How Did Father Die?	37
Koot Makes An Enemy	41
The Meat Chamber	46
Where Is Koot?	52
The Crow's Nest	57
Camels in Camp	61
Balancing Rock	66
Handprints on the Wall	71
Why Crows Are Black	74
The Red Fox	78
Teaching Tungo	84
Woman On The Mountain	89
The River Beckons	93
Tungo to the Rescue	98
Mother's Gift	102
Mark of the Mammoth	106
Tungo's Scatter Tool	111
Ona Hatches A Plan	117
Go Away, Koot!	121

The Long-toothed Cat   125
Basking In Glory   131
The Cat's Fang   134
Zol's Secret   138
The Stone Tooth   144
Star Dance   148
Preparing for the Hunt   156
Mammoth Hunt   159
Koot's Goodbye   166
Glossary   170

CHAPTER 1

THAT DREAM!

The Star Dancers circled the body, chanting the death song. Terrified, young Zol buried his face in his mother's tunic and wrapped his arms around her legs. Pressed so tightly against her, he could feel the animal sounds that convulsed her body and pierced the night air.

He peeked out just in time to see Yakono touch a flaming torch to the bed of dry branches beneath the body. Instantly the flames spread, as if alive, and hungrily licked at the naked flesh of his father.

"No!" screamed Zol.

Zol bolted upright, instantly awake. His heart raced like that of a frightened bird. Looking around, he saw familiar shapes in the darkness around him. He sank back onto his furs with a grateful sigh.

That dream again! He looked at the fur-covered humps next to him. His mother, grandmother, and sister slept soundly. Their bundled shapes did not move, and soft snores came from the hump that was Ona. Good. He had not cried out like a baby.

Many summers had passed since Zol's father had been killed by a mammoth. Why did the burning ceremony still haunt his dreams? Now that he was older, he understood what had taken place that night.

The Star Dancers *honored* their dead by burning the bodies this way. How else could the spirit of a loved one be set free to make its final journey into the sky and become a star?

As his heartbeat returned to normal, Zol gazed up at the night sky. The star people twinkled down at him now, as if to reassure him that everything was alright. It comforted him to know that his father— and all the star people—watched over them at night while Father Sun slept.

But Zol still ached for his father. He needed him now more than ever—to show him how to be brave. With a deep sigh, Zol pulled his furs tighter around him, rolled over on his side and drifted back to sleep.

Father Sun's brightness nudged Zol from a deep sleep. When he smelled wood smoke and heard the crackle from many camp fires, his eyes popped open. He was the only one still in his furs! He jumped up and pulled on his soft, elkskin pants and hide tunic. He had missed the morning greeting.

"Well, well," said his grandmother. "Our great hunter honors us with his presence." Ona sat hunched over the small cooking fire, her sleeping fur still draped over her shoulders against the morning chill. "Do you think Father Sun waits for you to awaken so the day can begin?"

She jabbed at the fire with her stick and frowned. "If you still need someone to shake you awake, then perhaps you are not yet old enough to hunt the mammoth after all." She squinted at him through the smoke of the fire.

"I'm sorry, Ona," said Zol, avoiding her piercing look. He hoped Father Sun would forgive him for missing the morning greeting. He reached for his line of bone hooks. "I'll go to the stream right now," he said. "It won't take me long to catch a branch of fish."

"Never mind," said Ona. "Lucky for us, Tungo has already been there and caught more than enough for his family and ours." She picked up a willow rack of freshly cleaned trout and wedged it with rocks so that it leaned toward the fire.

She sucked her upper lip in over her toothless gum and pulled her robe closer around her. "Tungo took pity on this poor old grandmother waiting for her morning meal. He threw me these fish as he went by, like you throw bones to a hungry dog!"

Zol's cheeks burned. There it was again—Tungo! He and Tungo were the same age of eleven summers, but Tungo hunted and fished like a man. Ona made no secret of her disappointment that Zol was not more like him.

Zol dropped to the ground, cross-legged, and took the bone cup of moss tea his grandmother offered him. His body felt like he had been trampled by a bison. He sipped the hot brew and looked around him. People were packing up, getting ready to move on. The Star Dancer clan had been walking north for many days, now, returning to their summer hunting camp.

Like the loons and the songbirds, Star Dancers moved south each cold season before the snows came. While Mammoth Camp lay frozen in winter's grip, they remained snug in hotus nestled among fragrant fir trees, in forests where the snows did not reach.

Zol shrugged his aching shoulders and looked at Ona. She was crankier than usual this morning and grunted as she moved stiffly around the campfire. She must be sore too, thought Zol. Even though her sharp words often stung him like bees, Zol respected his crabby, old grandmother. She worked hard. And she still carried her own belongings on the long treks between winter and summer camps.

The smell of fish sizzling over hot coals made Zol's mouth water. Mother came into camp carrying a camel hair net full of fresh, green balsamroot shoots to eat with their fish.

3

His sister, Keena, danced along next to Mother like a frisky young pup. Her fawn-skin tunic hung past her knees, and her black hair, tied in bunches at each side, bounced like tails when she moved. Only eight summers old, Keena's face was as round as the moon and glowed when she grinned, which she did now.

"Look, Mother!" she exclaimed. "Zol has already caught fish for our morning meal." She took the basket of leaves from Mother. "Mmmm, it smells so good...I'm starving!"

Mother squatted next to Zol to eat. She put an arm around his shoulders and gave him a squeeze.

"Hrmmpf," grunted Ona. "No thanks are due to this sleepyhead. Tungo has been our provider this morning."

Keena twisted a strand of black hair around her fingers. "Tungo was here?" she asked shyly.

"Yes," snapped Zol. "Showing off again!"

Ona grunted again, squinting her wrinkly eyes in the smoke as she removed the cooked fish from the fire and passed them around.

Zol bit into the crispy skin of the trout and tasted the sweet, moist meat inside. Juice dribbled down his chin, and he wiped it with the back of his hand.

Tungo. What did he know about living in a hotu without a father or brothers to help out?

As if he had heard Zol's thoughts, Tungo appeared out of nowhere and squatted next to Zol.

"Ho, Zol!" he said, punching him on the arm. "Good fish, huh?" He winked at Ona.

Zol winced. "Ho, Tungo," he mumbled. He wrinkled his nose at the body smell that was as much a part of Tungo as his loud voice.

Ona beamed at Tungo. "You are always welcome at our fire, young hunter."

"I can't stay," he said. "I'm loading the packs on the dogs. Yakono sent me to tell everyone to smother the fires and get ready to move. He says if we walk hard today, we can make it to Mammoth Camp before Father Sun goes to sleep."

4

Tungo jumped up and rubbed his hands together with delight. "Hoopa!" he shouted. "It won't be long before we'll be eating mammoth meat again! Right, Zol?" He gave Zol another friendly punch. Then he flashed a dimpled grin at Keena and ran off to the next campsite.

Zol sucked the last morsel of flesh from the backbones of his fish. He remembered his dream, and chills ran down his back like drops of icy water.

Mammoth Camp. Where Father had been killed. Where he, Zol, would join the mammoth hunt this fall. He threw the fish skeleton into the coals and watched it curl and blacken. He shivered. There was no turning back now.

CHAPTER 2

FATHER, I'M BACK

Zol struggled to keep the heavy load balanced on his shoulders. Finally he stopped and swung it down to adjust the hide straps. He straightened his burning shoulders and arched his back.

"Ahhh," he said, as the feeling of lightness washed over him. He could see his breath in the crisp, cold air. Yet his tunic stuck to him, damp with sweat.

Zol now carried half of Ona's bundle as well as his own. That morning, as he had watched his bent grandmother struggle to lift her heavy load, a sudden surge of pity had made him offer to help her carry it. She had refused at first, but when Mother flashed Zol a brilliant smile of gratitude, Zol had insisted.

"Move along, move along...you are slower than a slug!" Ona hobbled up behind him now, waving her walking stick in the air.

"You will never get to Mammoth Camp if you keep stopping like this," she said. "The last time I saw Tungo, that boy was running along with the dogs ahead of everyone."

"Tungo isn't carrying anything," said Zol hotly. "I'd be running too if I didn't have such a big load." Had she already forgotten that he was carrying her things as well as his own?

"Hrmmpf," Ona grunted and pulled her furs tighter around her frail body. No taller than Zol, she gave him a quick jab in the side with her stick as she hobbled past.

"Owk!" cried Zol. Anger flared hot inside him. It would serve her right if he left her things right here in a puddle. He started to untie her bundle, but the memory of his mother's warm smile that morning made him stop.

Shaking his head, Zol took another deep breath and hoisted the roll on his back. He looked ahead at the fur-clad figures moving in a single line up the greening hillside. He did not want to fall too far behind.

"Almost there...almost there," he chanted in rhythm to his steps. It was true, too, because in the distance he saw the big mountains of ice that never melt. His elk hide boots were soaking wet from the patches of snow on the trail and made a squishing noise with each step forward. He did not feel cold, though. Father Sun shone brightly today—a good omen. Zol felt his spirits lift, and a new burst of energy quickened his pace.

Suddenly he heard two sharp yelps followed by whimpering. Looking up, Zol was surprised to see Tungo and the dog sledges stopped in the trail right ahead of him. Tungo was furiously beating one of his dogs with a fat stick. The thin dog cowered at his feet.

Zol ran forward. "Tungo, stop it!" he shouted.

Tungo looked up, his wide face red with anger. "Mind your own business, Zol," he warned. "This dog sat down and would not pull anymore. I'm showing him who is the leader here." He raised the stick again, but Zol grabbed it and threw it away.

"Look at his load," said Zol, slipping his own heavy roll of furs to the ground. "This dog is pulling too much. You can tell by looking at him he's worn out."

Zol reached down and patted the quivering animal. The dog's pink tongue hung out the side of his mouth and his chest heaved with the effort of breathing.

"If you know so much about it, why didn't Yakono put you in charge of the dogs?" Tungo pushed his face up close to Zol's and glared at him with small black eyes.

Zol had no answer. It was true that their leader had given the dogs to Tungo's family to care for. It was not Zol's place to question Yakono's wisdom.

The Star Dancers each carried their own belongings on the trek between camps—sleeping furs, tool bags, and clothes. But the huge mammoth hides that stretched over their hotu shelters were too heavy for the people to carry. They were rolled up with the poles and tied to sledges that the dogs pulled.

"Here, I'll help you balance the loads," said Zol, bending to untie the hides.

Tungo shoved him away. "Mind your own business, Zol," he said again. "I'll take care of my dogs."

Zol shrugged and picked up his own load. "Oya," he said. "But remember, if you beat him to death, you'll have to pull the sledge yourself."

Forcing himself to walk on, Zol chanted again to drown out the dog's squeals. "Almost there...almost there."

At the top of the hill, Yakono raised his hand to stop. Mammoth Lake lay below them like a blue crystal sparkling in the sun. A thick tongue of white ice snaked through the grassy hills, coming to a stop at the north shore where it was slowly melting its milky color into the lake.

Yakono pointed to the spirit sign etched into the hillside across from where they stood. He raised his walking stick into the air with both hands and shouted with feeling, "Mother Mammoth welcomes us!"

SACRED
MAMMOTH SIGN

BALANCING
ROCK

ICE FLOW

PINES

WILLOWS

MEAT STORAGE

MAMMOTH
CAMP

N

The Star Dancers cheered.

Zol gazed once again at the incredible likeness of the brown mammoth that lay against the green hillside. The Earth's magic had caused mounds of lava to flow together and create a giant mammoth lying peacefully on her side, trunk raised in salute. The sight never failed to take Zol's breath away.

"Great Spirits!" he said in awe.

But then his eyes were pulled—against his will—to the Balancing Rock that perched at the very top of a hill near the south end of the lake. It was the scene of his terrible dreams—of the burning ceremony that he could not forget. It was where he had last seen his father.

"I'm back again, Father," he whispered. "And this time I need your courage."

CHAPTER 3
MAMMOTH CAMP

Mother and Keena held the mammoth hide in place while Zol fastened it to the poles with the bone pins he had made. Then he rolled heavy, round rocks up to the hotu and placed them around the bottom edges of the hide to hold it down and keep out the wind.

"There," he said at last. "Finished!" He flopped to the ground and leaned back against the hotu.

"You must be exhausted!" Mother said in a raised voice. "It is very hard to be the only male in a hotu of women." Her green eyes showered Zol with sympathy as she handed him a cup of sage tea.

Instantly feeling better, Zol took the cup and smiled at Mother. He knew she had spoken for Ona's benefit, and he was grateful. He did not want to hear again how Tungo had already been out hunting and snared the rabbit for their midday meal.

Zol was proud of Mother. Tall and slim as a birch tree, she walked with a straight back and graceful strides. Her face, always so serene, reminded Zol of the lake at evening. Her black hair hung in two thick, shiny braids that reached almost to her waist. And from the braids hung black and white feathers of the loon, her spirit sign.

Ona cleared her throat. She turned the browning chunks of meat that sizzled over the glowing coals. To Zol's surprise, she looked up at him and smiled. "My grandson has broad shoulders," she said. "He stands tall today."

A rush of pride surged through Zol. Suddenly he did not feel so tired anymore. He, Zol, was the man of this hotu. Mother and Ona had as much as said so! He sipped his tea, sighed in contentment, and looked around.

The Star Dancers were settling in at Mammoth Camp. People called to one another as they adjusted the tall, slanting poles of their hotus or tightened the hairy mammoth hides that stretched over them. Others hacked at the frozen ground with stone axes to deepen their fire pits.

A woman sang as she set up a drying rack in front of her hotu, and Zol heard a baby crying in the distance. Familiar, reassuring camp sounds—like every other summer. Only this would not be like every other summer for Zol.

Shaking the thought away, he stood up and said, "After we eat, Mother, I'll go scouting for some good chipping rocks for you."

Mother was known for her flintknapping ability—her skill at chipping stone points. And she was teaching Zol everything she knew. Zol's favorite times were when he and Mother sat together in front of the hotu, shaping pieces of colored chert or black obsidian into spear points and tools.

"Did somebody say rocks?" Tungo trotted into their camp, breathless and excited. "Hurry up and eat, Zol. Behind your Hotu, there's a tree full of crows we can use for target practice."

He swung his chunky arm around, pretending to sling a stone, and grinned. Then he turned his back to Keena and whispered, "It'll be fun because there's a nest of babies just getting ready to fly."

"Always hunting, that one," said Ona. She smiled at Tungo. "Would you like to eat with us, young man?"

Zol frowned. He was not sure he could even swing his tired arm in a circle right now, but he knew for sure that he did not want to listen to Tungo brag while he ate!

"I'm not hungry," said Zol. He reached inside the hotu for his sling and tucked it into his waist thong. "Let's go now."

As they approached the tall pine, they saw shiny black crows scattered around the top branches. In a nearby tree, adult crows cawed continuously, encouraging their fledglings to fly to them. The young crows hopped up and down and squawked—torn between fear and a desire to follow their parents.

"This is great!" shouted Tungo over the noise of the birds. He set a smooth stone into his sling. "Let's get the parents first."

As Tungo pulled his arm back to aim, a black fluttering at the base of the tree caught Zol's eye. It was a wounded baby crow.

"Wait!" he said to Tungo. He ran over and knelt on the pine needles by the thrashing bird. It was younger than the crows that were ready to fly. The way the wing was twisted under its body, Zol knew it was broken. The black, beady eyes looked at Zol in terror. He picked up the small body gently and cupped it in his hands.

He could feel its heart beating wildly against his palm. Even in its fear, the bird pushed against Zol's fingers with its tiny claws, struggling to get away. Tenderness welled up inside Zol for this terrified little bird that had never gotten the chance to fly.

"Sooo, soo," Zol cooed softly, touching the top of its head. "I won't hurt you." The bird began to relax.

Suddenly, Tungo reached over Zol's shoulder and grabbed the bird out of his hands. "Here," I'll wring its neck and get rid of it," he said.

"No!" Zol pulled at Tungo's arm, but the stocky boy shrugged him off and jumped out of reach.

Zol scrambled up and faced Tungo. "Give it back to me!" he demanded, holding out his hand.

Tungo clutched the struggling bird in his fist and held it over his head. "What's wrong with you, Zol? It's only a bird."

CHAPTER 4

A BABY CROW

"Zol, Mother wants—" Keena ran up to the boys. "Tungo! What are you doing?" she screamed.

Tungo whirled around at the sound of her voice. "Look what we found, Keena," he said, still clutching the bird tightly. "A bird with a broken wing." His face was flushed, as he held it out for Keena to see.

"Oh, the poor thing," said Keena in a soft voice. "Did it fall out of its nest?" She touched the baby crow's head, and Tungo loosened his grip.

Zol snatched the bird away from Tungo. "Here, Keena," he said. "Why don't you take it back to camp and see if you can mend its wing?"

Keena's large brown eyes lit up. "Oh, do you think I could?" she looked at Tungo through her dark lashes. "Thank you, Tungo," she said sweetly. She turned and ran back to camp, cupping the crow carefully in her hands.

"Come on," said Tungo gruffly. "Forget the crows. I'll show you where I found some snowshoe rabbits yesterday." He took off in his heavy-footed trot without looking back.

Zol followed, running effortlessly in long, graceful strides over the soft bunchgrass. Masses of yellow balsamroot blossoms rioted against the hillside like splashes of sunshine. Here and there, huge granite boulders sat alone, looking out of place on this grassy steppe.

Great Spirits! He loved to run. Sometimes Zol felt like he could run forever. He liked the feel of the wind washing over his body, liked the sound of his feet slapping the ground. He could think better while he ran.

And now he thought about the boy running next to him. Zol knew he should be more like him. Tungo *lived* to hunt. For Tungo, animals were there to kill; meat to eat and fur to use. If they were not edible, they were target practice.

That is the way a Star Dancer *should* feel, thought Zol. How could the clan survive without the meat and hide of animals? His own father had been a great hunter; if he were alive today, he would expect Zol to follow in his footprints.

But surely animals felt fear and pain too. He could not forget about that; it haunted him!

Without breaking stride, Zol jumped onto a speckled boulder in his path and leaped into the air. If he had wings, he could fly! But he landed on the bunchgrass, instead, still running.

He looked over at Tungo, as they ran, and shook his head. He could never be like Tungo. They were as different as night and day. Zol was tall and slight, like Mother. Tungo was short and thick through the middle, like his brothers—and strong! Zol's black hair swung neatly at his shoulders, while Tungo's thatch of coarse hair stuck out in all directions, like a crow's nest.

More importantly, Tungo had already proven himself as a hunter, while Zol was clumsy with snares and missed the mark more often

15

than not with his sling-stones. He realized that he would rather carve animal shapes from wood than hunt for them.

Zol made a decision right then. He would try harder. He would watch Tungo and try to be more like him.

Tungo stopped at the top of the hill, panting. "Look!" he pointed to a meadow on the other side.

Zol looked. He saw bunchgrass, sagebrush, clumps of balsamroot and blue camas flowers. He would tell Mother about this place, so she and Keena could bring their digging sticks and collect the camas bulbs.

"Can't you see them?" asked Tungo, staring at Zol. "They're everywhere!" He whipped out his sling and stooped to pick up some round stones.

Finally, Zol's eyes caught movement, and he saw what Tungo saw: snowshoe rabbits in their blotchy spring coats. They were hopping around under the sagebrush, feeding on the grasses and sedges.

Snowshoe rabbits were white in the winter, when snow covered the ground, and they had huge hind feet that let them walk on top of the snow. Now, they were growing their summer coats of reddish brown fur, which would make them harder to see in the summer.

Tungo ran forward, swinging his loaded sling over his head. He stopped short and hurled the stone. It found its mark, and an unlucky rabbit that had been sitting on its haunches, curious about the two-legged creatures, slumped silently to the ground and lay still.

"Hoopa!" shouted Tungo, fitting another stone into his sling. "Hurry, Zol, before they get away!"

Zol fumbled for the sling he had tucked in his waist thong. He set a round stone into the cup-shaped piece of hide and, holding the long narrow straps together by their ends, he began twirling it over his head. But somehow, he let loose of one of the ends too soon, and the stone went flying off to the side. He scrambled to fit in another stone but, in his rush, did not place it right, and it plopped to the ground at his feet before he started twirling it.

By this time, Tungo had already brought down another hare, and the rest had scattered for cover.

"Sacred Mammoth, Zol! What were you waiting for?"

"I...I..." Zol hung his head in shame.

"Wait until Ona hears about this," snorted Tungo. He tucked his sling under his thong and ran to get his catches.

Holding them by the ears, he faced Zol. "There were so many hares, it was hard to miss!" He shook his head and shoved a rabbit at Zol. "Come on, let's go back to camp and skin these. I have to give the meat to my mother, but you can take the skins to Keena. My mother has too many."

Zol knew what Tungo was doing: taking the skins to Keena meant he would have to explain to Ona why there was no rabbit meat for stew.

But when Zol reached the hotu with the skins, Keena saved him from an explanation.

"Come and look, Zol!" She pulled her big brother into the hotu. Proudly, she showed him the cage she had built out of pieces of camel bone tied together with hide strips. On the bottom was a nest made from dried moss and lined with a scrap of rabbit fur.

Resting in the cozy nest was the baby crow. One wing stuck out from its side. Keena had cut a tiny splint from a willow twig and wrapped the wing to it with soft strips of sinew.

Zol grinned at Keena. "Did you do this by yourself?"

Keena nodded. "Mother showed me how. She says I can keep him only until he can fly." Then she twisted her hair around her finger and looked up at Zol through her lashes.

"Will you help me feed him?" she pleaded with her doe's eyes. "I told Mother you would."

"Crows in camp are bad luck!" said Ona from the doorway.

Zol and Keena jumped at the harsh tone in her voice.

A fierce scowl deepened the wrinkles on Ona's pinched face. "They bring death," she growled.

She folded her arms over her chest. "Crows are birds of death, I tell you. Get rid of it!"

CHAPTER 5

WHAT GOOD IS A CROW?

Mother pulled aside the door flap and stepped inside. "It is only a baby," she said, "and I would like Keena to try and mend its wing. It is good practice for her."

She put a hand on Ona's arm. "Remember, not all Star Dancers believe as your mother's people did."

"Useless!" said Ona. She turned and stomped outside.

Zol slivered bits of fresh rabbit meat from the skins with his sharp obsidian blade and chopped them into tiny pieces. Then he showed Keena how to be a mother crow, by poking the meat into the bright red mouth with the blunt end of a bone needle.

"See, this needle is like a crow's beak," said Zol. But he soon found it was not that easy. He was afraid of hurting the baby bird by pushing too hard; and if he did not poke it in far enough, the meat got stuck halfway.

Finally, the hungry crow and the determined boy got the hang of it. Working together, they got enough food down to satisfy the black bird's hunger.

Keena dipped her fingers into a bowl of water and let the baby crow take drops into his beak. Then the bird closed its eyes and slumped down into the nest, fast asleep.

"What shall we call him?" whispered Keena.

"Why not wait to see if he survives?" said Mother gently. "He may have more injuries inside."

Keena's eyes clouded up. "He won't die, will he?"

"The way he gobbled down that food, I doubt it," said Zol.

"We will know more tomorrow," said Mother, "and if he lives, you will see how hard it is to be parents of a demanding baby." She steered them toward the doorflap. "Now come, you two. Ona has our meal ready."

Before light the next morning, Zol heard the crow hopping in its cage. He peeked over at the fur lump that was Keena, but she did not move. The crow began to peck noisily at the bone cage and made funny little noises to itself that sounded like "cu-koot, cu-koot."

Zol raised himself on his elbow to look. As soon as the crow spotted him, it scrunched down, threw back its head and screeched, "aawk! aawk!" while fluttering its one good wing.

Zol laughed. "Shhh, little one, you'll wake up the whole camp." He reached for the strip of pemmican he had been munching last night. Full of crushed nuts, dried berries and animal fat, pemmican was what the Star Dancers lived on during the long cold winter months when they could not get fresh meat. He guessed it would be good enough for the crow.

He broke off small pieces and poked them down the bird's throat until it was quiet again. Then Zol sank back into his furs and drifted off to sleep, dreaming of black crows flying in big circles against a brilliant blue sky.

Zol and his family were just stirring in their furs when Tungo pushed aside the heavy hide doorflap, letting in a whoosh of cold air.

"Hoopa!" he said with a silly grin on his dirty face. He shoved a speckled grouse in ahead of him, dangling the plump bird by its legs. "I've caught your morning meal for you," he announced proudly, looking at Keena.

"Ripe camel dung!" muttered Zol. "Don't you know it's still dark out, Tungo? How can you be hunting already?"

"I found the grouse nest yesterday," said Tungo eagerly. "I knew if I got there early enough, I could just reach in and pick up the hen. I got all her eggs too," he said, "but I gave those to my mother."

"Smart boy," said Ona, scrambling out of her furs to take the bird from him. "Now *there* is a provider for you." She glared at Zol. "He does not waste his time saving useless birds."

Zol wished Tungo would leave, but the boy stood there grinning and basking in Ona's praises.

"Come look at the crow," said Keena. She sat up, clutching her fox sleeping fur around her against the cold morning. Her black hair hung loose around her face.

"Later," said Zol sharply. "Come on, Tungo, if you're going to stay, let's build up the fire and start the water boiling." Quickly, he pulled on his pants and tunic.

"Why *are* you wasting your time on that dumb crow?" asked Tungo as they hauled water from the lake in hide boiling bags.

"It's fun," said Zol. "It's like having a pet...you know, like you get to have the camp dogs."

"But my dogs are important to the camp," said Tungo. "There's a reason to have them. What good is a stupid crow that can't even fly?"

Zol shrugged. "I don't know," he admitted.

Maybe Tungo was right. Maybe Zol should have let him kill it on the spot.

CHAPTER 6
THE SPEAR-THROWER

Tungo and Zol slurped hot moss tea and chewed noisily at the grouse bones to get every bit of tasty meat.

"Let's practice with our spear-throwers this morning," said Tungo, talking around a leg bone in his mouth.

"My brothers told me about a good place to go, just a short run from here. It's called Stony Creek. We can practice throwing and then look for chipping rocks." He frowned. "I'm almost out of spear points, and my brothers won't give me any of theirs."

"Good for them," said Mother. She was kneeling on the ground, helping Keena peg one of the rabbit skins for scraping. "Before you can call yourselves hunters, you boys must take responsibility for making your own tools."

She smiled at her son. "Zol, you know the kind of fine, smooth stones I like. Would you look for something with color in it for me?"

Zol looked into Mother's smiling green eyes. Mother was the best flintknapper in the Star Dancer clan. It was because of her skill at chipping points that Yakono had allowed her to keep her own hotu after Zol's father was killed.

Mother made her powerful points for all the best hunters in the clan, which gave them more time to scout and hunt. Many hunters believed that Mother's skill with the stone came from Earth's magic, and that she breathed powers into the stone as she worked it.

Zol smiled at that because he had inherited her skill. She was teaching him everything she knew. Great Spirits, he loved to chip and carve!

"Oya," said Zol. "Maybe I can find some of that clear crystal rock." He pointed to Keena's pendant.

His sister looked up and touched the bird shape she always wore around her neck. Zol had chipped it in such a way that sparkles of color shot out from the wings whenever Father Sun smiled on it.

"I would love that!" Mother exclaimed. "Get going now, you two. And practice hard, so we can be proud of you when you join the hunters this fall."

Zol's heart skipped a beat at the thought.

But Tungo grinned from ear to ear. "Hoopa!" he said, rubbing his hands together. "I'm almost as good as my brothers already."

Grudgingly, Zol had to admit he was right. And most boys in the clan were like Tungo. They could barely contain their eagerness to join the mammoth hunters. It was the high point of a Star-Dancer's life; when he became a man. What was wrong with Zol, that he dreaded it so?

At campfires, even the faded eyes of elders danced again with boyish delight when they told stories about their first mammoth hunts.

Something was wrong with Zol, he was sure of it. He dared not tell anyone, but the rubbing on of Father's ashes had not worked—he was actually *afraid* to join the hunters!

Zol jumped up to shake away his thoughts. "Let's go, Tungo. I'll get my spear-thrower."

They slung their tool bags over their shoulders and took off at an easy trot across the grassy plain dotted with sagebrush.

It was easy to spot Stony Creek on the open steppe. The icy stream gushed out of a huge pile of boulders and carved a narrow channel across the grassland. Along both banks, spindly water birch stood tall above the tangle of low-growing brush, while golden willow branches hung over the stream, ready to send forth their new green leaves.

The boys scooped up drinks of water in their hands, then leaned back against a flat rock to rest from the run. Tungo picked up Zol's spear-thrower. He tested its balance and ran his hands over it. Then he looked at Zol with that gleam in his eye that Zol had learned to dread.

"Want to wrestle for your spear-thrower?" he asked. "No!" said Zol, pulling it away from Tungo. "I spent too much time working on this. Make your own."

Tungo always wanted to wrestle because he was good at it. He was strong, and his short, stocky build made him hard to throw down. Zol had many memories of being thrown to the dirt by Tungo in a blink of an eye.

"Come on," Zol said, standing up. "Let's start throwing."

"Wait," said Tungo, pulling him back down. "What are you afraid of, huh?" His voice got whiny. "Even if you lose it, you can make another one."

Zol ran his hand over the smooth, shiny wood of his spear-thrower. He had searched for days before finding the perfect branch of chokecherry to use. With his stone axe, he had chopped off a piece the length of his arm. Then, with his stone carving knife, he had scooped out a hand grip on one end of the stick.

On the other end, to hold the spear, he had carved a hook. With the blunt end of the spear jammed into the hook, or nocked up, Zol could easily hold both the spear and the thrower at the same time.

Finally, he had polished it smooth with sandstone and beaver fat before winding thin strips of hide around the handle for a sure grip.

Tungo shoved his roughed-out spear-thrower into Zol's hands. "Look, this isn't so bad. It's almost done. It would be easy for you to finish...and who knows? Maybe you'll win!"

They both knew there was little chance of that.

Zol looked down at Tungo's sad piece of work. It was as crude and unfinished as most of his stone points were. "Great Spirits, Tungo!" said Zol. "You can sit patiently at a rabbit hole for most of the day, but you don't have the patience of a grasshopper when it comes to making your tools."

Tungo snorted. "Maybe mine doesn't look as good as yours, Zol, but maybe it works better." A sly grin spread across his face.

"If you don't want to wrestle, let's see who is better at hitting the mark." He fingered the big cat tooth he always wore on a thong around his neck.

"Tell you what," he said. "If you win, I'll even give you my cat tooth." His small eyes gleamed. "I plan to get more of my own, anyway, after I join the hunters."

Father Sun danced off the white fang that lay against Tungo's brown chest. Zol had envied it ever since Tungo's brothers had killed one of the long-toothed cats, two seasons ago, and given the fang to Tungo.

Zol knew he would never have a better chance to gain such a treasure. After all, he *had* been practicing with his spear-thrower, and his aim was improving.

Tungo sensed Zol's hesitation and jumped up. "Come on!" he said. "I'll make the target."

He ran over to a large willow tree, opened his tool bag and took out his axe. He gashed at the brown bark until he had exposed a large area of lighter wood underneath. Then he took a piece of red ochre from his sack and colored an oval shape in the center. He stood back, pleased with himself, and rubbed his hands together.

"That's the heart," he called to Zol. "You go first."

Zol had been backing away from the creek, deciding just how he wanted to make his run at the tree. Now he slipped his right hand into the hide strap of the grip. He took one of the short spears that dangled at his waist and nocked it up by fitting the butt end into the hook of his spear-thrower. Holding on to both the thrower and the spear, Zol drew his hand back until his elbow was even with his right ear.

Concentrating on the target, he took a deep breath and started running. When he was close enough, he thrust his arm forward, letting the short spear fly with a snap of his wrist. He watched the spear slice through the air on a true course and heard the "thung" as it found its mark. "A heart hit!" he yelled.

Tungo went to the tree and yanked the spear out. "Lucky hit!" he called. "My turn now."

Zol could almost feel that cat tooth around his neck. He had never thrown better! He practically danced to the bushes at the stream's edge to watch Tungo set up for his turn.

As he watched Tungo back away from the tree, Zol heard a deep growl behind him. Whirling around, he stared into the fierce, yellow eyes of a grey wolf as tall as Tungo!

The snarling wolf curled its upper lip and bared its teeth. Seeing its bloody snout, Zol realized instantly that he had surprised the animal in the midst of eating a fresh kill.

An icy chill shot down Zol's back. His heart pounded. Wolves were ferocious when defending their kills. He would have to kill this animal—or be killed himself!

His hand tightened on his spear-thrower. He tried to reach for a short spear at his waist. But he could not move! The wolf's angry eyes held Zol captive with their intensity. He could not breathe!

The wolf crouched and started toward him.

Like a tree, Zol stood rooted to the spot.

CHAPTER 7
WOLF DREAMS

A vicious snarl, as the wolf sprang, snapped Zol out of his trance. He crouched and covered his head with his arms. Something whizzed past his ear. He heard a strangled yelp as the wolf landed on him, knocking him to the ground. The smell of warm animal fur filled his nostrils. He was still alive! He opened his eyes and stared directly into the glazed open eye of the wolf.

"Aauugh!" screamed Zol. The wolf's limp body lay on top of him, nearly covering him. Its mouth hung open and its pink tongue draped over Zol's shoulder. Something warm was seeping through his tunic; it smelled like blood.

Quickly, Zol struggled to push himself out from underneath the dead animal. One of Tungo's short spears stuck out of the wolf's chest. Zol felt dizzy and sick to his stomach.

"Yazoo!" shouted Tungo, throwing both his arms and spear-thrower into the air. "I did it! That really *was* a heart hit!" He bounded across the grass to Zol.

"Why did you just stand there like a tree?" he asked. But he did not wait for an answer. He knelt over the wolf and pulled out his spear.

Shame washed over Zol. He tried to stand, but his legs would not hold him. What good was it to make beautiful spear points and throwers when he did not have the courage to use them when it counted? Tungo's crude tools had saved his life, while he stood there unable to move.

"Thank you, Go Go," Zol mumbled, calling him by the baby name he had used when they were little.

Tungo looked at Zol strangely. "Sacred Mammoth! You're as white as birch bark! You weren't afraid of that old wolf, were you?"

"No! I just couldn't get my short spear untangled from the thong," lied Zol. He grabbed Tungo's arm. "Listen, don't tell Mother and Ona how I bungled this...oya?"

Tungo's expression suddenly changed. "Oya," he agreed. He wiped his nose with the back of his hand and said, "I won't say a word to anyone. But, Zol, I *did* win your spear-thrower, didn't I?" His eyes held Zol's.

Zol's heart sank, but he nodded. He knew how hard it would be for Tungo to keep this to himself. Zol was just glad he had something to trade for the boy's silence.

"Hoopa!" shouted Tungo. "This is my lucky day." He opened his tool bag and took out his large obsidian, skinning knife. "Wait until my brothers see this hide—it's a beauty!"

He bent eagerly to the job of skinning the wolf. "My mother needs a new sleeping fur; this will be just right." He grinned at Zol, the disgrace already forgotten. "I'll come back with a sledge for the meat, but I want to take the fur now."

Zol nodded and tried to make his voice sound normal. "I'll go look for the chipping rocks that Mother wants," he said.

Relieved to be getting away from the wolf scene, Zol ran to where the stream bubbled over a pile of rocks. He splashed the cold water on his face and gulped it from his cupped hands.

The water chuckled and seemed to mock him as it rushed over the slippery rocks. A painful ache pushed against the back of his throat, as he threw water on his face to hide the tears running from his eyes.

What if Keena or Mother had been with him instead of Tungo? Zol shivered to think about it. It was his job to protect his family—Yakono had told him so—and Zol could not even protect himself!

A flock of crows circled overhead, calling noisily to each other. It was obvious they had spotted the wolf carcass. Remembering the baby crow back in camp, Zol began to feel better.

By the time the boys got back to camp, Zol had recovered. He carried chunks of reddish-brown chert and several large moss agates that he knew would please Mother. Tungo's happiness at bringing back both a wolf hide *and* Zol's spear-thrower was contagious. Zol almost believed their story that he had not seen the wolf until Tungo shot it.

Keena ran to greet them. "I fed the baby crow all by myself," she boasted to Zol. Then she saw the silvery hide that Tungo carried on his shoulder and her eyes got big. "Oooh, Tungo! What a pretty fur!" She ran her hands over it.

Tungo had been sagging under the weight of his burden, but at the sight of Keena, he stood straighter and let the fur unroll. "You should have seen me, Keena," he began, "I made a perfect heart-hit."

Zol gave Tungo a meaningful look and left him with Keena to brag about his kill. Setting down his load of rocks, Zol went into the hotu to see the crow.

When the baby bird saw Zol, it squatted down, fluttered its good wing, and threw open its red mouth to be fed. "Scrawk!" it cried.

Zol laughed for the first time that day. He picked up the scruffy little crow and cupped it in his hands next to his face.

"Did you miss me, little bird?" He rubbed the crow against his cheek. "I think Tungo gave some of your family a big feast today...but I wasn't much help."

The crow gurgled in a low voice as if he understood. Then he pushed against Zol's hands and said, "cu-koot, cu-koot" in that funny talking way.

"Cu-koot yourself," said Zol, setting the bird back in its cage. He broke off a piece of dried root cake and shoved it down the crow's throat.

"Cu-koot. Maybe that's what we should call you—or just Koot. Yes, I like that better. You look like Koot...what do you say to that?"

The crow stretched up tall. Then he cocked his head to one side. "Caw!" he said, making a little hop. Smiling, Zol closed the cage and went back outside.

Tungo was already repeating his wolf story to Ona. Zol watched his grandmother's wrinkled brown face. Admiration poured out of her bright eyes as she listened to Tungo's tale, which got more exciting with each telling.

Nights were still cold enough to keep a small fire going inside the hotu. That night, wrapped in his furs, Zol watched wisps of smoke drift lazily up through the opening at the top of the hotu. Uninvited memories of the wolf encounter pushed into his thoughts. Zol rolled over and tried to shake them away.

He heard loons calling to each other on the lake. Then another sound floated in on the night air: a low, mournful wolfsong. Soft at first, the howling grew louder until it filled Zol's head. Was it the grieving mate of the dead wolf?

As terrified as he had been, Zol admired the wolves. They were like the Star Dancers. They traveled in packs, mated for life, and killed only when they needed to eat or defend their own.

Zol knew that the first Star Dancers had learned from the wolves how to bring down the mighty mammoth. Hunters had studied the way wolves watched a herd of bison—sometimes for days—until they knew which of the huge animals was weakest. Then, working together, the wolves drew that animal away from the herd, surrounded it, and brought it down. If it worked for the wolves, reasoned the elders, could not the Star Dancers hunt an animal many times *their* size in the same way?

And it worked! To this day, in gratitude for those lessons, the Star Dancers always left part of a mammoth kill for their wolf brothers.

The haunting wolfsong rose and faded in the night, mingling with the cries of the loon. Then, in the distance, a chorus of wolves answered.

Zol buried his head in his furs to block out the sound.

CHAPTER 8

SACRED MAMMOTH

"Is there something wrong with your eyes, that you cannot see a wolf as big as a hotu?" Ona squinted at Zol through the drying rack they were setting up. Strands of wispy, grey hair hung over her brown face.

Zol knew what was coming. He had managed to avoid being alone with Ona for days, but this morning he was at his grandmother's mercy. Mother had taken Keena to the lake to gather fresh willow shoots for baskets. And she had asked Zol to stay and help Ona.

"My back was turned, that's all," said Zol. "He crept up on me."

"Hrmmpf. The wolf has not been born that could sneak up on your father or my brother, Yakono." Ona never let anyone forget that she was Yakono's sister.

"You should spend more time practicing like Tungo does," she continued. "You waste too much time chipping stones and carving wood; women can do that."

She jabbed a bony finger in Zol's chest for each point she made. "*Hunting* is what keeps us alive. *You* are the man in this hotu. It is your *job* to hunt!"

"Scrawk!" screeched Koot from his cage next to Zol.

Ona sat back on her haunches and frowned at the bird.

Keena had quickly tired of the crow's constant demands for food, so it now fell to Zol to care for him. He liked doing it; the bird made him laugh.

Zol had brought the cage outside with him today, and now he was thankful. The bird gave him a reason to interrupt Ona. He got up and went to find some tree grubs for Koot.

"So now that useless bird is more important than helping your old grandmother?" Ona spat. "Pah! Your mother is too soft with you."

Zol ignored Ona's words and brought wiggly morsels back to the crow. "Hello, Koot," he said, as he always did when offering the bird food.

It had not taken Koot long to learn that those words meant something good was coming. He squatted down, fluttered his good wing, and threw open his mouth.

Zol laughed when the crow swallowed greedily—making little noises—then opened up again for more.

Koot was growing fast. It kept Zol busy, these days, catching crickets, tree grubs and other insects to shove down that gaping gullet.

"Foolish! A foolish waste of time!" Ona threw down the willow branches she was tying and glared at Zol. "You should be spending time hunting for *us*—food for *our* bellies—not picking worms off of trees for a bird we will not even eat!"

Zol took the cage back inside the hotu. "Koot," he said softly, "I think you'd better stay inside today." He put his hand in the cage and stroked the crow's beak.

"Cu-koot, cu-koot," answered Koot, closing his eyes in obvious enjoyment.

Zol went back outside and picked up the branches Ona had thrown down. He began tying them together with strips of elk hide. It was going to be a long morning unless Zol could think of some way to distract Ona from his failures. If he could just get her started telling a story—.

"Are you listening to me?" Ona's crackling voice broke into his thoughts. "I asked you to hold this section while I tie it. But again you are off in your dream world. Is that where you were when Tungo was alert and ready to kill a wolf?"

"I was thinking about the Sacred Mammoth sign, Ona." Zol silently thanked Mother Mammoth for giving him the perfect distraction. "Tell me again how our people found this place...I love that story."

Ona's eyes softened. She grinned, exposing her pink gums. She loved talking about the old times. Carefully, she set down her section of the drying rack and looked at her grandson.

"Many, many seasons ago," she began in her story-telling voice, "when I was still a baby on my mother's back, the great spirit of the Mother Mammoth led us here."

Looking at the deep wrinkles in her face, Zol could not imagine Ona as a baby—or even as young as Keena.

"It was a bad time," she said. "It had not rained for many seasons. Everywhere we looked, nothing but sand and dust. There were no plants...no grasses." Ona shook her head.

"Our men went out every day, searching for the meat we so desperately needed. Sometimes they found a skinny rabbit or a squirrel, but the mammoths were nowhere to be found. All the grazing animals—even the elk—had disappeared."

Ona wrinkled her nose. "We even sank so low as to eat the foul-smelling camel meat! Thank Mother Mammoth I was still nursing then!" She shuddered. "They eat garbage, you know."

Zol laughed. He and Keena loved to watch the funny camels that wandered into camp from time to time. But nobody ever thought of eating them! On the other hand, it was great good luck to come across a pile of bleached camel bones from a cat kill—or of one that had died of old age.

The hard bones were prized by the Star Dancers and eagerly divided up among them. Zol himself already had a complete set of camel toe bones.

"Then one day two of our scouts came upon an ice bridge over that angry river below us," continued Ona. "They wanted to cross, but they were afraid. The ice bridge creaked and groaned and dripped.

"If it broke while we were crossing, we would all be lost." She made a sweeping motion with her hand. "—swept away and smashed between the boulders and jagged chunks of ice that tossed and tumbled below us."

Zol shivered at the thought of trying to cross that river! It still frightened all of them with its power.

"My father was the leader then," said Ona. She leaned forward and squinted her deep-set eyes at Zol. "He took my big brother, Yakono, by the hand, and started to walk across that creaking, cracking ice without looking back."

She sat up slowly and pursed her lips, letting her words sink in. "Nobody would follow. My mother cried and wailed as if her heart would break, but she was too afraid to follow. All the people stood there like trees and watched those two brave men disappear. We thought they were gone forever."

A faraway look crept into Ona's small dark eyes. "That is how it happened that my father and Yakono were the first ones to see the mammoth sign."

Suddenly, Ona set her willow strips down and struggled to her feet, leaning on Zol. She reached for her walking stick. "Come!" she commanded. "I want to see the spirit sign now."

They walked to the lake in silence and sat on a fallen tree. On the other side of the lake, facing them, the Sacred Mammoth lay soaking up the warmth of Father Sun.

Large brown hills of lava shaped the mammoth's head and body, while smaller bumps and gullies formed its legs and trunk. Cloud shadows played across the form, making it appear to be alive and breathing. A line of dwarf birch trees—bright green with new growth—curved gracefully around the trunk like a tusk.

"This is the way they found it that day," said Ona in a hushed voice. "My father told me that the mammoth sign beckoned to him with her trunk as if to say, 'Come, I will feed you.'"

No matter how many times he had heard the story, this part always gave Zol a little thrill.

Ona pointed. "You see where the trunk is pointing? My father looked up there and saw the great wall of ice, blue in the distance. He knew in his heart that the mammoth was telling him to go there. So he took Yakono by the hand, and they walked toward the ice."

Zol held his breath, even though he knew what was coming next.

"They walked and walked and walked. But the ice seemed to be no closer. Then my father saw them: brown spots in the distance. A herd of mammoths grazed peacefully on the tender, green bunchgrass that grew in front of the ice wall. My father sat down to rest, and tears of joy ran down his face. His people had been saved!" Ona stared at the sign, as if in a trance.

"But how did he make the rest of you cross the ice bridge?" asked Zol. Even now, sitting half a day away from the river, they could hear its crashing roar.

"He simply walked back over the bridge," said Ona, "and told the people, 'I have found the mammoth.' Then he took my mother by the hand, turned, and started back over the river again."

Ona poked Zol. "Remember, I was on her back! Oh, how my mother wailed in fear! But he was a strong leader, my father, and the people followed."

Ona's eyes sparkled at her grandson. "My brother, Yakono, is such a leader today." She paused. "And the blood of these leaders runs through you."

They sat silently, staring at the Sacred Mammoth. Yes, thought Zol, the blood of courage runs through me. So why do I not *feel* it?

He looked over at Balancing Rock and the low burn slab next to it. Father, he implored silently, why are you not here to lead *me* by the hand?

CHAPTER 9
HOW DID FATHER DIE?

Zol and Mother sat outside the hotu chipping stones. They each had a piece of bison hide draped over their legs for protection against the sharp stones. As he expected, Mother was happy with the rocks he had found for her.

Times like this, when the two of them worked together on stone, were rare now. Mother was too busy teaching Keena how to find roots and plants or how to scrape animal hides clean to make soft clothing.

She was preparing Keena to keep a hotu of her own, just as she had taught Zol how to make stone tools for hunting. Zol understood, but he missed his time spent alone with Mother.

Koot ran busily between Zol's and Mother's legs. He picked up colorful rock chips that caught his fancy, and then he fluttered away to hide them. He loved colorful, shiny objects. Zol chuckled at the crow's happiness.

Koot's wing was almost healed now, and he exercised by flying around inside the hotu. Unfortunately, his antics had been causing trouble.

Nothing inside the hotu was safe from Koot's prying, poking beak. He loved to pull the laces out of Ona's boots and tunic, which made her angry. So today Zol had brought him outside to explore.

Mother turned over a chunk of reddish chert in her hands. "I think this will need to be hardened in the coals to make it easier to knap," she said.

She knocked off a flake. "See how it does not want to hold a sharp edge?" she handed the piece to Zol, and he could see it did not have the glassy sheen of obsidian or the gloss of the dark piece of flint he held in his hand. "Later, I will show you how to bury these pieces under coals in a fire pit," she said. "In a few days they will be perfect for working into points."

They continued working in silence, except for the musical clink of stone against stone as they broke open rocks with their hammers. Zol's elkhorn hammer felt comfortable in his hands. It had belonged to Father and was Zol's most prized possession.

He looked at Mother. Her shiny, black hair was parted neatly in the center, and her thick braids hung forward as she bent over her work. Against her knee she held a long piece of cream-colored agate, which she was making into a knife. The tip of one braid touched the back of her hand as she pressed the antler tine into the rock to remove a flake. She tossed the braid over her shoulder and saw Zol looking at her. She smiled.

"Mother," said Zol, "how did the mammoth kill Father?" He saw pain shoot into her eyes, but he had to know. The question had been haunting him.

"Why do you ask, Zol?"

"Because ever since I was little, I have been told what a great hunter Father was, and how it was such a tragedy the way he died. But when I ask exactly *how* he was killed, everyone changes the subject. Even Yakono just shakes his head and says, 'such a waste.'"

Mother looked down at her hands, which lay still now. Zol took a deep breath and continued in a rush, "I remember the way Father's body looked that day the hunters brought him back to camp." The next words caught in the back of his throat and made a funny croaking noise.

Too clearly he remembered the bloody tangle of arms and legs that had once been his hero. The high-pitched wails of his mother and grandmother had filled the air, piercing Zol's ears and heart until he thought he would explode. His laughing father, who used to throw him into the air and catch him in strong arms, lay in a broken heap before him.

Mother looked at him now, her eyes brimming. "Oh, Zol!" she cried. "I hoped you were too young to remember."

She reached out her hand and touched his arm. "It was an accident, Zol, a strange accident." She squeezed his arm. "Of course I will tell you.

"The mammoth had arrived as expected that season," she began. "And because of your father's hunting skills, Yakono let him choose the animal they would go after. Father studied the herd for days. He was good at spotting the weaker animals—those that could be brought down quickly with spears."

She paused, as if trying to decide how to continue. Unexpectedly, she smiled. "After he had chosen the animal, he made a paste of powdered red ochre and melted fat. He watched and waited until that mammoth was grazing off by itself. Then he crept up behind it and rubbed the red paint on its back legs."

Zol gasped, but Mother laughed. "Everyone thought he was so brave," she said, "but the shaggy beast did not even know he was there. I myself was watching. Mammoths have very poor eyesight, you know, and Father made sure to stay downwind so the beast could not smell him."

Her green eyes widened. "Nobody had ever marked a mammoth before. It was Father's idea. He thought if everyone could watch that particular mammoth and learn its ways, there would be less fear and tension on the day of the hunt."

Zol gazed at the elkhorn hammer in his hands—once held by the very hands that had dared to mark a mammoth!

"And it worked," continued Mother. "The hunters sat and watched that mammoth for days, from a safe distance. They became familiar with its habits. They talked and planned. When the day came to attack, the hunters were confident and excited. They were not afraid."

"Then what happened?" asked Zol.

"The day of the hunt, they watched the marked mammoth as usual. They knew it often lagged behind the others—it had been injured, you see. So they waited until the herd had wandered ahead of it. Then they crept up close to it."

Mother's hand tightened on Zol's arm. "Just as your father dashed in to jab the first spear into the soft underbelly, the mammoth chose that moment to roll in the dirt.

"At the very moment your father thrust the spear into its belly, the mammoth lowered its hind legs, driving the wooden shaft into Father's chest and crushing him under its huge body."

She closed her eyes briefly. "The others quickly finished the mammoth off from all sides with their spears, but it was days before they could get to Father's body." She took a deep breath. "I cannot say more, now."

That night, rolled in his furs, Zol looked up through the smoke hole at the star people. One bright star—bigger than the rest—twinkled at him.

"Father, can you hear me?" he whispered. "The ashes did not work, Father. I did not receive your courage!"

Zol held the elkhorn hammer close to his beating heart. His father's fearless hands had shaped it. Had Father's courage also soaked into it? If he squeezed hard enough, would Father's bravery seep into him?

Squeezing the hammer, Zol stared at the twinkling star until his eyelids got heavy. Finally, he slept.

CHAPTER 10

KOOT MAKES AN ENEMY

Smoke rose from the smoldering ashes as the Star Dancers hummed a mournful tune and circled the stone slab. Someone began to shake a hollow bone filled with animal teeth; others joined in with a slow, steady rhythm.

Zol clutched Mother's tunic. Her wailing grew louder. Suddenly, strong arms pulled him away from her. "No!" he screamed, reaching for his mother.

Yakono carried Zol toward the burn slab, toward the pile of smoking ashes that had once been his father.

Zol struggled to get away. "No!" he cried.

———————

Zol sat up, his heart pounding against his chest. The darkness of the hotu comforted him, and he sighed with relief. That dream again! He realized he was still gripping Father's elkhorn hammer.

41

Was Father's spirit trying to reach him in the dream? Zol put the tool down, slipped out of his furs and quietly went outside to relieve himself. It was almost dawn, but he could still see the stars. "What am I going to do, Father?" he asked.

But any answer he might have received was interrupted by a rattling noise inside the hotu. Zol smiled. Koot was trying to get out of his cage. He should have known he could not sneak out of the hotu without waking Koot.

The crow was growing stronger every day and wanted to be with Zol at all times. Zol realized that Koot thought he was his mother. It felt good to have this wild bird greet him with such happy excitement each day.

Zol slipped back inside and sat on his furs. He opened the cage, and Koot hopped out. Zol fed him some pemmican to keep him quiet. Koot hopped onto Zol's shoulder, gurgling and cooing in the boy's ear. To Zol, it sounded just like the crow was talking.

Koot hopped onto Zol's head and started preening the boy's shoulder-length hair with his beak, just as he preened his own feathers.

"Hey," whispered Zol, "what are you doing? Do you think I'm a crow, too?" Zol took Koot outside. This was as good a time as any to teach the crow how to find crickets for himself.

After the morning greeting, Zol sat inside the hotu, carving fish hooks out of elk antler. Keena was playing with camel bones and Koot was poking around Ona's furs.

"Zol," Keena warned. "Look what Koot has found."

Zol looked up and saw Koot working at the drawstrings of Ona's fawn-skin pouch, which she kept under her pillow fur. Suddenly the pouch opened and the contents spilled out onto her furs.

Koot screeched when he spotted one of Ona's most prized possessions—a polished piece of clear amber. For the crow, it was love at first sight. He snatched the amber piece and strutted around the hotu with the bright stone in his beak.

Zol and Keena laughed. "I'd better take it away from him before Ona gets back," said Zol, getting up.

At that very moment, Ona pushed back the doorflap. She shrieked when she saw Koot with her gem. She rushed inside and lunged at the crow. "Give me that, you thief!" she shouted.

But Koot easily avoided her grasp and flew up to where the poles crossed at the top of the hotu.

"Caw-aw, caw-aw." He stared down at Ona, the stone firmly clamped in his beak. It looked like he was laughing at her. Then he dropped the stone. As Ona ran for it, Koot swooped down, scooped it up again, and returned to the top of the hotu poles.

Ona shook the poles and screamed at him; she threw her moccasins at him. But Koot stayed where he was, as if deliberately teasing her. Zol knew he should do something, but it was too much fun to watch.

Finally Ona gave up in frustration. She put her hands on her hips and looked up at Koot. "You evil bird! If you dare swallow my amber piece, I myself will wring your neck and cut it out of you." She glared up at him.

As if in answer, Koot dropped the stone right on her forehead. Zol and Keena howled with laughter, rolling on the furs and holding their sides. Ona glared at them, then snatched up her amber and marched from the hotu.

Zol put Koot back in his cage while Keena put Ona's things back in her pouch and under her pillow. Zol tied the cage with two hide thongs, each with double knots. He could hear Ona outside, talking to Mother.

"I tell you the truth," said Ona. "Keeping a crow in camp is bad luck! His wing is healed; it is time for that nasty bird to fly."

"Now you've done it," said Zol to the crow. "Ona didn't want to keep you in the first place. I'd better go out now and apologize to her."

"Caw-aw," said Koot, immediately starting to peck at the knots. Zol added a third knot.

When he stepped outside, Ona had already left in a huff to see Yakono. Zol sat on his flat rock to carve more fish hooks and wait for her.

He was surprised to see her smiling when she came back. She carried a large chunk of mammoth meat. Fatty and tender, mammoth was Ona's favorite meat. The few teeth she had left were getting loose, and the dried strips of elk and bison were hard for her to chew.

Ona begged and traded—even gambled with camel bones—to get tender hunks of meat. When she was successful, it made her feel like she was still contributing to her daughter's hotu.

"My brother has sent a message to you," said Ona. "He wants you and Tungo to meet him at the meat chamber today when Father Sun is directly overhead."

A little thrill shot through Zol. Working at the meat storage chamber was man's work.

"Thank you, Ona," he said, grinning at her. "Did you win that meat at camel bones or did Yakono give it to you?"

She sat down with a little grunt from the weight of the meat. "My brother still cares for his sister," she said. She narrowed her eyes at Zol. "He does not laugh at her distress."

"I'm sorry for what Koot did, Ona." It was hard for Zol to keep a smile from his lips. "I've tied Koot's cage with two thongs. I don't think he'll be able to escape and find your amber."

He stood and brushed antler chips from his pants. "I'd better run and find Tungo."

"That is right, my grandson," she said, under her breath. "Your crow will never again touch my amber."

Zol heard her mumbling, but did not pay attention. He did not see the determined look on her face as she watched him leave.

CHAPTER 11

THE MEAT CHAMBER

The meat storage chamber had been dug out many seasons before Zol and Tungo were born. It was a large, egg-shaped pit dug into the permafrost as deep as the frozen ground would allow.

Many large boulders—each weighing more than two men—had been rolled and pushed into place around the edges. Smaller rocks filled the gaps between the boulders, making a tight rock wall around the pit—except for one hole that was just big enough to crawl through.

Trees had been cut and laid over the top, then covered with more rocks and dirt. Finally, a heavy door-stone had been chosen to place over the entry hole to keep out hungry bears and wolverines. It took three men to open and close the chamber.

When Zol and Tungo arrived, the door-stone had already been moved aside. They peered into the dark chamber, and a cold, musty smell greeted them. It was empty, and nobody else was around, so they sat on the ground by the entrance.

Tungo wore something new around his neck above the cat tooth: two shriveled round things that hung on a string of sinew. They looked vaguely familiar to Zol.

"What is that around your neck?" he asked.

Tungo grinned and picked up the yellowish balls. "Wolf eyes," he said.

Zol's stomach did a flip-flop. "Great Spirits! Why are you wearing them around your neck?"

"Animal eyes have powers," said Tungo. "My brother told me so. Now I'll be able to see like a wolf at night."

He got up on his knees and stuck his head inside the chamber. "Eecch! It stinks in here!" He pulled his head out and made a face at Zol. "And I think Yakono is going to make *us* clean it out."

"If we have to clean it, maybe that means they've spotted the mammoth herd already," said Zol. A shiver ran down his spine.

"No, my brother Nuba went with the scouts yesterday," said Tungo. "They haven't spotted anything yet." He frowned. "I don't see why I can't go with them—I've got *good* eyes." He sat back on his haunches and fingered his wolf eyes. "I'll bet I can see better than those old scouts!"

"It takes more than good eyes to be a scout, Tungo." The deep voice made both boys jump and whirl around. Yakono had come up silently behind them. Now he towered over them, blocking out Father Sun. "A good scout also knows when to keep quiet."

In spite of his many seasons, Yakono dropped easily to a cross-legged position on the ground facing the boys. "Thank you for arriving so promptly," he said. "That is the mark of a good hunter—to be ready *before* the animals come, not running after them as they leave."

Zol stared at their leader. Nobody knew how old he was, but Yakono knew everything there was to know about the Star Dancers. Zol thought he must be as old as the trees.

Yakono had a wide face with high cheekbones set far apart. He still had all of his teeth, and he had more wrinkles on his face than anyone Zol had ever seen. Even his large ear lobes were wrinkled! The short hair on top of his head was caught up in a tuft that stood straight up, bound with a red cord.

Yakono's proud look commanded attention, and the red band of ochre painted across his forehead told everyone he was their leader.

"I have an important job for you boys today," he said in his deep voice. "This storage chamber must be thoroughly cleaned out and dug even deeper."

Seeing Tungo's disappointment, he added, "It is an honorable task that has been performed by every hunter in this band. It is the first step you will take toward becoming hunters for the Star Dancers. Caring for this chamber is as much a part of successful hunting as is making a good spear-thrower."

Tungo shifted uncomfortably, and Yakono looked at him. "Do you know why, Tungo?"

Caught off guard, Tungo said, "Why what?"

Yakono frowned. "Why is it so important to clean the storage chamber properly?"

Tungo twisted his cat tooth nervously. "So it will be clean?" he asked more than answered.

"And why should the chamber be clean?" persisted Yakono.

Tungo looked at Zol, his eyes begging for help.

"Long after the thrill of the hunt is over," said Yakono, "the meat from the sacred mammoth will sustain the Star Dancers. It will keep us alive when we return to this sacred place and hunt again." He turned his intense black eyes to Zol.

"We are a small band of small people in this great land. We are not as mighty as the mammoth—either in strength or numbers. Yet Mother Earth has given us the magic to bring down that great beast in order to feed ourselves.

"Think of it! We do not have long fangs, like the big cat. Nor do we have sharp claws like the bear. Yet we are able to eat mammoth meat. Is this not truly amazing?" He nodded solemnly, as if answering his own question. "This ability is a gift, and we must use it wisely. Do you agree, Zol?"

Zol nodded. He had never thought of the mammoth hunt like that. Compared to the mammoth, a Star Dancer was like a bird on the back of a bison. Great Spirits, thought Zol. We do not even have the great speed of the wolf! How do we dare?

"So," continued Yakono, "which one of you will tell me why what we do today is important to all the Star Dancers?" His eyes held Zol's, so the boy felt compelled to answer.

Zol swallowed, hoping he would not sound as dumb as Tungo. "Because we are a small tribe, and even if we kill only one mammoth, it is too much meat for us to eat all at once."

"Exactly!" said Yakono, smiling for the first time. "The mammoth is a gift, and we must not waste it. After a successful hunt, we will make many trips back to camp with loaded pole sledges.

"We will fill this chamber with meat and close it. Then the frozen ground and cold nights will make the meat hard and keep it from spoiling."

He turned to Tungo. "There is another reason," he said soberly.

Tungo twisted the tooth with both hands. "Uhh...maybe there will be some left in the chamber when we come back next summer?"

"Wonderful!" thundered Yakono, making Tungo jump. He put a hand on Tungo's shoulder. "We were lucky this past season; winter was short. Our supply of dried meat lasted until we headed north. We are not always that lucky.

"Many seasons we arrive at Mammoth Camp hungry and weak. Frozen mammoth meat waiting for us in a well-kept storage chamber can mean the difference between life and death."

He looked at both boys for a long time in silence, as if trying to decide if they were capable of the task before them. Tungo fidgeted.

Finally, Yakono said, "It is a big job; that is why you must start now. I myself will work with you today and show you what I want you to do. After today, I expect you to come here every day at this time and work until Father Sun hangs low over the mountains. Now let us go to work."

Yakono taught the boys how to strip large sheets of birch bark from the trees and lay them on the bark side so the edges curled up. Then he instructed them to scoop up armloads of the blood-soaked pine needles that covered the floor of the meat chamber in a thick layer. This they piled in mounds on the birch-bark "sledges." When the bark was full, Yakono led them to a gully far away from camp, where they dumped the loads.

"The smell of blood will draw wolves and cats," explained Yakono, "so it is important to take the old needles far away. Sometimes just the smell of the open chamber draws unwelcome visitors."

He looked at Tungo. "Tomorrow I want you to bring two of the camp dogs with you to stand guard outside while you work." Tungo puffed up with importance and smirked at Zol.

Working on their hands and knees in the cold pit, the boys scooped and hauled the smelly, soggy pine needles until Zol thought he would drop from exhaustion. The sharp needles poked his cold skin, and his arms and hands were full of red welts. His feet felt like chunks of ice...he could not wiggle his toes. Worse, he had to listen to Tungo complain the whole time.

Finally, Father Sun began to sink toward the hills. Zol and Tungo eagerly left the chamber. They tried to move the door-stone over the entrance, to keep out unwanted animals, but they could not budge it. Tungo ran off to get his father and brothers to help him.

On his way back to camp, Zol stopped at the lake to wash his blood-soaked tunic. Crows scolded him from a cluster of pines, and Father Sun warmed his bare back as he scrubbed the hide shirt with rocks.

He watched a family of black-headed geese paddle lazily toward him with fuzzy goslings in tow. The proud parents held their heads high, showing off their white chinstraps. Zol smiled. The baby geese reminded him of Koot waiting for him at the hotu. He looked forward to resting and playing with his crow.

Back at the hotu, Zol laid his wet shirt on the flat rock to dry in the sun. Then he went inside to see Koot. Something was wrong: no squawks or screeching for food greeted him. Zol looked at the cage. The thongs were untied, and Koot was gone.

CHAPTER 12
WHERE IS KOOT?

"Ona!" shouted Zol, throwing aside the heavy doorflap of the hotu. "Where's my crow? Where is Koot?"

Ona stirred the fire and did not look at him as she answered. "It was time for that bird to fly," she said.

"What do you mean?" asked Zol. A painful knot formed in the back of his throat. "What did you do?"

"All I did was show him the outdoors," said Ona, "and he flew away without even looking back. A crow is not a dog, you know." She raised her head to look at him now. "He does not have feelings of loyalty. And besides that, crows are bad luck."

Zol felt his face get hot. Trying to swallow the knot in his throat, he choked, "How could you do that to me, Ona? He was *my* crow! *I* wanted to be the one to let him go. I knew it was time for him to fly, but *I* wanted to be the one to set him free!" He was shouting now, and his vision blurred. "Now I'll never see him again. How could you *do* that, Ona?" Tears escaped his eyelids and he brushed them off his cheeks.

"Look at our big man-hunter, crying like a baby over a bird!" Ona pursed her wrinkled lips. "Your mother is too soft with you. You do not have time for that kind of silliness now."

At that moment Zol hated his grandmother; she sat there so smug, stirring the fire. He wanted to throw something at her. He ran back into the hotu, pulled on another tunic and dashed out again. "Which way did he fly," he demanded.

"I do not know," said Ona, pouting. "I did not care to watch him."

Zol had to get away from his grandmother. He ran blindly toward the river and did not stop until he had a pain in his side and was gasping for breath. Then he flopped down under some pine trees and leaned against a tree trunk to catch his breath.

He gave in to that pressing ache in his throat and sobbed. When he finally stopped crying, he saw that Father Sun was almost gone behind the mountains. The sky blazed with red and orange streaks as far as he could see. Soon it would be dark and Koot would be alone.

Zol knew that crows in the wild roosted together in big family groups. But Koot did not have a crow family...he only had Zol. What would he do? Would he be able to find food for himself?

Zol could see the raging river in the distance and hear its roar. Even from this distance, he could see the huge chunks of ice that dashed along in the wild current. Sometimes the angry water tossed a whole tree into the air and sucked it down again. Zol shivered.

As he watched, a large cloud of crows flew toward him from the west—probably heading for their roosting tree. Against the sunset, the black cloud swirled, rose, and settled again, as if one mind controlled all the birds. Would Koot ever be part of a crow cloud like that?

Zol cupped his hands over his mouth and shouted, "Caw! Caw!" trying to imitate Koot's call. His voice carried into the evening wind. "Hellooo, Koot!" he called. He knew his voice wo uld be eaten up by the roar of the river, but it felt good to shout. "Caw! Caw! Hellooo, Koot!" He called again and again until his voice cracked.

Father Sun slid behind the mountain and disappeared. The sky turned a deep pink, and Zol stopped calling. He just sat there watching the day fade away.

"Caw! Caw!"

Was Zol hearing things, or was a single crow calling from somewhere far behind him? He jumped up and turned to face the sound. With the wind behind him now, Zol called again, "Hellooo, Koot! Caw! Caw!" He was not sure, but he thought he heard an answering call. He did not dare to believe it!

Then he saw a crow hopping, more than flying, from tree to tree toward him. "Koot!" screamed Zol, running toward the bird. And before he had gone more than ten steps, the crow glided down to his shoulder and awkwardly grabbed onto the hide tunic.

Zol put the bird on his hand and brought it around to face him. "It really is you! Oh, Koot, you found me!" Zol was so happy, he wanted to squeeze him, but instead rubbed his cheek against the crow's shiny wings. Koot gurgled and cooed. When the greeting was over, the bird hopped up Zol's arm, squatted down, and screeched for food with his beak wide open.

"So that's why you found me," laughed Zol. "Ona was right; it isn't loyalty...you just got hungry!" He found a sharp stick and dug for grubs and worms to satisfy the young bird's hunger. Then, with Koot riding proudly on his shoulder, Zol trotted all the way back to camp. It was dark, and he knew Mother would be worried.

"Mother! Keena!" shouted Zol, when the shaggy hotus were in sight. They came running to see what was wrong.

Keena clapped her hands. "It's Koot! You found him!" she squealed.

When Ona saw Zol walk into camp with Koot on his shoulder, she gasped. She slapped her hand over her mouth and ran into the hotu. In a few minutes she came out again, carrying her pot of red ochre. On her face she had painted a ring of red around her mouth and both eyes. She had rubbed the red around her ears too.

"See what I told you," she said ominously to Mother. "That bird is bad luck. Bad luck always returns until it has its way." She shoved the ochre pot toward her. "Here, protect yourself against the evil—quickly!"

"Do not be afraid," said Mother, smiling at Ona's old beliefs. "Koot is just a young bird who thinks Zol is his mother. When he was hungry, he searched until he found his mother...just like any young animal would."

But Zol's grandmother would not be swayed. She believed what she had learned as a child. "Until that bird of death leaves, I am going to protect myself," she stated firmly, sucking in her upper lip, "and you are foolish not to do the same. Come here, little one." She grabbed for Keena, but the little girl slipped out of her grasp and ran to her mother.

Zol ran his hand over Koot's sleek feathers. He saw Ona's real fear of the crow for the first time, and it surprised him. "At least she will not try to get rid of you anymore," he whispered to the bird. "But just to be safe, tomorrow I'll make a roost for you in one of the pine trees."

Zol returned Koot to the cage and moved it closer to his furs. That night he slept with his fingers curled around the camelbone bars.

CHAPTER 13

THE CROW'S NEST

News traveled fast among the small clan of Star Dancers. Tungo was at Zol's hotu the next morning right after the morning greeting.

"Is it true that you called your crow right out of the sky?"

Zol heard the awe in Tungo's voice. And for the first time ever, it was directed at him!

"My father says you must have special powers," said Tungo, "to call a bird out of the sky like that."

Ona dropped a hot rock—sputtering and steaming—into the boiling bag over the fire. "Listen to me," she said. "It is the *bird* who has special powers. Stay away from that bird, young man, if you know what is good for you."

The boys ignored her. "Will you help me make a roost for him in the trees?" whispered Zol. "I'm afraid to leave him in the hotu anymore." He pointed behind his hand to Ona.

"I will if you'll show me how to call him out of the sky," said Tungo with a sly smile. "That's one thing my brothers can't do."

After the morning meal, Zol and Tungo went to the willow thicket by the lake and collected what they thought were the makings of a nest. They had seen many crows' nests high in the pines. From below they just looked like a jumble of twigs and sticks woven together with bits of sinew, mammoth hair and hide scraps.

"How hard can it be?" asked Zol. "If a bird can do it with only a beak and claws, surely we can figure out how to do it with our hands." They sat with their pile of materials under a pine tree close to Zol's hotu.

Koot perched on Zol's shoulder and cocked his head with interest as the boys tried to weave together a nest for him out of the sticks and twigs. Time after time, they would think they had done it, only to have the whole mess fall apart at the slightest touch.

"Caw-aw-aw," said Koot, and it sounded just like he was laughing.

"I don't see you jumping in to help," said Zol, rubbing his cheek against the bird affectionately. "You should be the one doing this, not us."

Koot jumped down into the pile, picked up a long willow stick in his beak and danced back and forth with it. Then he flew up into the pine tree.

"He understood you!" said Tungo. His black eyes were as round as rabbit holes. At that moment, Koot rattled his laughing sound and dropped the stick right on Tungo's head. "Owk!" said Tungo, rubbing his head.

Zol laughed. "I don't think he likes you," he said. "That's what he does to Ona."

Tungo's voice got whiny. "I want him to like me," he said. "Show me what to do."

"Watch," said Zol. "Hello, Koot," he called to the crow. At once Koot swooped down and landed on Zol's shoulder. Turning to Tungo, Zol said, "Say 'hello, Koot' and see what happens."

"Hello, Koot," said Tungo. But Koot just stretched one leg, then the other, and fanned his tail. "Hello, Koot!" repeated Tungo like a command. This time Koot squawked at him and nibbled at Zol's ear.

"Here," said Zol, "put out your hand and I'll hand him to you." Zol took Koot off his shoulder and set him gently on the back of Tungo's hand. "Now talk to him softly," instructed Zol.

"What should I say?" asked Tungo. "I feel silly talking to a bird." He brought his hand closer to his face, and Koot stepped back and forth nervously. "Why is he staring at me like that?" asked Tungo.

All of a sudden, Koot darted his head forward, shoved his beak inside one of Tungo's nostrils and yanked the tiny black nose hairs.

"Owk-owk!" yelped Tungo. At the same time, he brought up his other hand and slapped Koot to the ground. "You stupid bird!" he shouted.

Koot screeched and flew into the tree again. But he glared down at Tungo, stepping from one leg to the other.

"Uh oh," said Zol. "Now you've done it. He's not used to being treated like that."

"Well, what did you expect me to do?" whined Tungo, rubbing his nose. "That hurt. How would you like it if he stuck his sharp beak up your nose?"

"That's just the way he shows affection," said Zol laughing. "He was just preening you. Sometimes he sticks his beak in my ear...it just tickles, if you don't let it scare you."

Still watching Tungo from above, Koot started scolding. He jerked his head back and forth with every "kawk!" and "kuk!" and continued to glare at Tungo.

Zol laughed again. "Look, he's really mad at you! I think you hurt his feelings."

At that moment Koot swooped down onto Tungo's thatch of matted hair and pecked him once—hard—before hopping over to Zol's shoulder. Zol laughed so hard at Tungo's surprised expression that he fell over backwards. Koot flew back into the tree.

Tears jumped into Tungo's eyes. "That's not funny, Zol." He scrambled to his feet, covering his head with his hands. "I think Ona's right. I think that bird is evil."

Because Zol was still laughing, Koot started his rattling laugh-sound too, and Tungo was furious. He kicked the pile of twigs. "Make your own roost...I don't want any part of that bird. I'll see you later at the meat chamber—and leave the bird at home!" Tungo turned and ran, stumbling over a log as he rubbed his head.

CHAPTER 14
CAMELS IN CAMP

Quietly, Zol lifted the flap and stepped into the frosty morning. The sky was that deep dark blue that happens just before light—that time of day when grassland creatures begin to stir. Crickets were singing a slow song, and an occasional killdeer called out.

Zol inhaled the morning air. It smelled fresh and sweet—like damp sagebrush. The day would be clear and sunny, but now it was still cold. Zol pulled his bisonhair robe closer around him. He wanted to check on Koot.

Zol had given up trying to make a nest for the bird. Instead, he had taken the old piece of rabbit fur out of Koot's cage and climbed with it as far up the pine tree as he could. Koot flew around him the whole time, squawking, as if encouraging Zol to fly with him. Zol had found a perfect depression where one of the branches joined the trunk, and there he had placed Koot's fur, making it stick with pine sap.

"There," he told the squawking bird. "That's your roost."

He had placed Koot on the fur, gently stroking him and talking softly as Father Sun left the sky. The bird's eyes would close, but as soon as Zol shinnied to the ground, Koot was right there on his shoulder. Zol could not make him understand that he had to stay in the tree.

Finally, in frustration, Zol had thrown the crow into the tree roughly and said, "Stay there, Koot!" He had walked away without looking back, and he had worried all night.

Now, in the pre-dawn light, he stood at the base of the tree looking up at the dim tangle of pine boughs. He could not see where he had placed the fur.

"Koot," he called softly, "are you there?" He heard a slight rustling, but no answering gurgle. Maybe Koot's feelings were hurt. He would wait until he could see better before climbing up to look.

Zol looked around him at the sleeping Mammoth Camp. For the first time he understood the wisdom Yakono had shown in choosing this spot. They were on a rise, so they could see great distances in all directions; yet their hotus were nestled in among the trees of a pine grove. The pines gave each hotu some privacy and protected them from the winds that blew constantly over the grassy steppe land.

They were close to Mammoth Lake, which gave them clear water and sweet fish. But they were high enough to escape the cold rush of air that blew off the ice wall at the head of the lake when Father Sun went to sleep.

The lake also drew animals to its shore to drink—animals the people could eat, like deer and elk and pigs. Yes, Yakono was a wise leader. And Zol was lucky to be learning from such a great man.

Zol returned to the tree. "Hello, Koot," he called again. And again came the answering rustle, but no call. The camp was beginning to stir. The sky was lighter now, and Father Sun was on his way. It was almost time for the morning greeting.

Zol caught some grasshoppers for Koot's breakfast. A pink glow made him look up at the sky, and he gasped at its beauty. It looked as if someone had taken a fox tail, dipped it in berry juice and dabbed

62

it all over the wide sky. Color was everywhere. He started toward the hotu to wake Keena, but had only gone a few steps when he heard, "Caw!" Looking back, he saw Koot's black form circling over the roosting tree. "Caw! Caw!"

Zol's heart thrilled at the sight of that familiar black form gliding in circles higher and higher into the glowing pink sky. For the first time since arriving at Mammoth Camp, Zol felt glad to be alive. Somehow Koot's presence made Zol forget the nagging fear that usually lurked in the corners of his heart.

"Hellooo, Koot!" he called. Without hesitation, the crow flew toward him, folded his wings and dropped out of the sky; he made tighter and tighter spirals until he landed on the ground in front of Zol. Then he hopped onto Zol's shoulder, nibbled his earlobe and gurgled into Zol's ear as if to say all was forgiven.

Zol hugged him to his cheek and said, "I'm so glad to see you, Koot. Stay on my shoulder, now, and please be quiet during the morning greeting. Don't do anything to make Ona mad, oya?"

Zol fed his crow the grasshoppers he had caught, one by one, until Koot was satisfied and settled down to preen his feathers on Zol's shoulder.

Mother and Keena came out of the hotu, followed by Ona. Keena was rubbing the sleep from her eyes, but when she saw Koot on Zol's shoulder she clapped her hands. "Oh, Koot, you're alright!" She ran toward Zol.

"Shssht! Children!" hissed Ona, pinching her narrow, brown face into a frown. "Have you no respect?" She glared at Koot.

Mother gave them a meaningful look too, so Zol and Keena obediently took their places next to Mother, who already had her hands raised, palms up, to the eastern sky. They all faced the bright glow that fanned out in an arch above the dark ridgeline. They began humming, just as Father Sun peeked over the ridge—a small ball of light which grew rapidly in size and intensity until they could no longer look at it, but had to bow their heads. The warm sunlight washed over them like a blessing.

63

The sound of humming from all the hotus lifted into the morning air, and Zol felt the vibrations all through his body as he gave himself over to the greeting. Lost in the moment, he was only dimly aware that Koot had turned on his shoulder and was stepping back and forth from one leg to the other.

Zol felt Keena's hand in his, tugging at him. He opened his eyes to see her grinning and pointing. There, just below them, was a group of camels. Everyone knew that camels liked music; they had probably been drinking at the lake and were attracted by the humming. Many of the elders felt that camels in camp ensured the coming of the mammoth, so their coming was always greeted with pleasure.

The Star Dancers encouraged the awkward camels to stay around the camp by throwing their garbage where the camels could get to it easily. Camels would eat just about everything, and their dried dung around camp meant that the children did not have to go far to collect fuel for the campfires. Also, the bunches of long woolly hair they shed were eagerly gathered by the women for making ropes and nets.

"Oh look," whispered Keena, tugging at Zol again. "They have a baby with them!" They watched a clumsy little camel, all legs and knobby knees, nosing around under its mother's belly to nurse. The mother swung her long neck around to look at her baby, then turned back and continued tearing at the bunchgrass with her sharp teeth.

All this time Koot was getting more agitated and curious. He had never seen a camel and before Zol could stop him, he flew over to the funny-looking animals with the humped backs. On the ground, Koot strutted and waddled from one animal to the next, as if looking the situation over. Finally he stopped in front of the mother camel and pecked at the shiny nail-shaped hooves on her cloven feet. She stared at him through large dark eyes framed with long lashes. Then she squealed and stepped back awkwardly.

"Hey, you stupid bird, get away from the camels!" Tungo ran to shoo Koot away.

Tungo had never shown much affection for animals, so Zol was surprised to see him so worried about the camels. By the time Tungo reached the camels, Koot had flown up to the mother's hump. He began preening the camel's long brown hairs as if he were preening his own tail feathers.

The camel looked up in surprise. She turned her head to look at the crow on her back, and the way her upper lip was split, it looked like she was smiling at him.

People were coming from all the hotus now, gathering around to see the camels. Zol saw Tungo place a large stone in his sling.

"Tungo, No!" he yelled, running to stop him.

Tungo twirled the sling around and around, as he turned to Zol. "The camels are more important to this camp than your evil crow," he shouted. "Look at what he's doing...he's going to drive them away."

"Koot is not hurting her," said Zol, grappling for Tungo's arm. "Give me that sling. You'll kill him with such a big stone."

"No!" said Tungo. "I'm going to show that bird some manners."

He jumped back, away from Zol and closer to the camel. At that moment, the irritated mother camel brought her head around, laid back her small ears and spit a mouthful of green, slimy cud at Tungo. He was so shocked that he just stood there with his mouth open, while the bad-smelling ooze dripped down his face. The camel stared at him haughtily, her whiskered face serene.

Koot stretched up tall, flapped his wings and made his laughing noise. The Star Dancers, who had been watching the whole thing, started to laugh too.

Tungo's face turned bright red, and his little eyes were black slits when he hissed at Zol, "That does it. I'm going to kill that bird!" He turned and marched away, wiping at his face with the sleeve of his dirty tunic.

Suddenly Yakono was at Zol's side. "Come with me, Zol," he said. "We must talk."

CHAPTER 15

BALANCING ROCK

Zol followed his leader toward the lake in silence, and his heart fluttered when he saw where Yakono was headed. Without a word, Zol followed him up the steep hill to the Balancing Rock. There, Yakono stooped and ran his fingers over the broad, flat granite stone next to it, which was sooty and blackened from many burning ceremonies. Then he turned to Zol and motioned for him to sit.

Zol's heart pounded in his chest as he dropped cross-legged to the ground. What were they doing here? This was a *sacred* place.

Yakono sat next to him and examined his sooty fingertips before speaking. "I myself rubbed the ashes from your father into you," he said. He took Zol's arm and drew a black line with his finger on the boy's copper skin. "While your father's ashes were still warm, while his courage was still present in them, I myself rubbed them into your head, your heart and your hands. Do you remember?"

Did he remember! Zol had relived that night in his dreams again and again. He nodded silently.

"I have been watching you, Zol. And what I see makes my heart heavy. Your father's blood runs through you. His courage has been transferred to you in the ashes. It is time now for you to take your father's place in our clan. But something holds you back."

Zol felt hot tears well up behind his eyes, and he struggled to keep them from spilling over.

Yakono put his big hand on Zol's shoulder. "What troubles you, my son?"

Zol could no longer hold back the tears. "It didn't work!" he blurted out. "The ashes didn't work! I do not have the courage of a Star Dancer. I...I'm *afraid* to go on the mammoth hunt!" He felt the tears starting down his cheeks.

Yakono removed his hand and clasped it with the other one between his knees. Silently, he and Zol watched a flight of honking geese land on the blue lake below them. Puffy, white clouds drifted in a sky the color of a robin's egg.

Zol swiped at his tears and waited for his leader to speak.

Finally Yakono said, "Look carefully at the Balancing Rock. What do you see?"

Zol looked at the huge granite boulder. It did not sit on the ground the way boulders normally do, but sat instead on a smaller piece of rock that jutted out of the ground beneath it. The giant boulder was bigger around than ten Star Dancers standing side by side. It was taller than a mammoth. But the little rock on which it sat was no bigger than a rabbit. How it stayed balanced like that was a great mystery to the Star Dancers.

"I see a big boulder on top of a little rock," said Zol.

Yakono nodded. "What do you think keeps this boulder from rolling off the little rock and down the hill into the lake?"

"Magic?" asked Zol.

Yakono smiled. "Balance *is* like magic," he said. "If that boulder had been set one finger-width forward or back on the little rock below it, it would have rolled down the hill and disappeared into

Mammoth Lake. But Mother Earth wants it there; she set it there, and so it stays there." Yakono was silent again, staring at the Balancing Rock as if deep in thought.

Then he said, "We Star Dancers are like this boulder, Zol. We, too, are balanced on the earth. Mother Earth wants us here. She keeps us here by giving us plants and berries to eat, water to drink, and animals to hunt."

Yakono placed his hand gently on Zol's shoulder again. "You must not be afraid of the mammoth, Zol. She is what keeps us alive and balanced on this earth. Do you understand what I am saying?"

Zol was not sure he did, but he nodded anyway.

Yakono pointed to the ground under the Balancing Rock. "See those chips of rock around the base? The little rock is chipping away, piece by piece. Some day, when enough rock has chipped away from the little rock, it will no longer be able to hold this big boulder in place, and the Balancing Rock will roll down the hill to be swallowed up by Mammoth Lake.

"The Balancing Rock does not worry about that day. It greets Father Sun every morning like we do, throwing its shadow across the grassland." He turned to Zol and fixed him with his deep-set dark eyes. "Do you know why we choose to have our burning ceremonies here?"

Zol shook his head. "No."

"To remind us that our lives are balancing like that boulder. When it is our time to fall, we fall...it is nothing to fear. But you are here now, Zol, and while you are here it is your job to hunt food for your clan."

"Caw! Caw!" They both looked up to see Koot circling above them. Zol looked at Yakono questioningly. The leader nodded yes.

"Caw!" answered Zol through cupped hands. The crow spiraled out of the sky and landed on Zol's shoulder. He started gurgling into Zol's ear, but Zol brushed him off his shoulder, afraid that Yakono might be angry at the interruption. Koot flew to the Balancing Rock and started stretching and preening his black wings.

"Koot is a fine crow," said Yakono, smiling, "in spite of what Ona says. It is impressive the way you can call him out of the sky. But now it is time for him to take his place with other crows—just as it is time for you to find *your* own place with the Star Dancers."

The leader's face became serious again. "That bird is causing too many angry words between you and your grandmother. And it has come between you and Tungo at a time when you boys should be working together." Yakono stood up. "I have faith in you, Zol. I know that when the time comes, you will do the right thing." He patted Zol on the shoulder and turned to walk down the hill and back to camp.

Koot immediately flew over to Zol's head and began preening the boy's black hair. Zol put his arm up, and Koot hopped onto it. He brought the crow down in front of him and looked into the dark, beady eyes staring at him.

"I don't have to prove myself to you, do I, Koot?" He stroked the bird under the chin, and Koot stretched up and closed his eyes, gurgling his contentment.

Zol sat there by the Balancing Rock for a long time, petting his crow and thinking. Finally he said, "Yakono is right, Koot. It is time for me to learn how to be a brave hunter, and time for you to leave me and find a flock of your own."

With a quick glance at the burn slab, Zol got up and started running down the hill. Koot spread his wings and flew next to him all the way back to camp.

CHAPTER 16

HANDPRINTS ON THE WALL

Zol and Tungo worked side by side on their hands and knees in the cold meat chamber. Tungo barely spoke to Zol; he was still angry at being humiliated in front of everyone. Surprisingly, though, Tungo had kept his word and not told anyone about Zol's shameful failure with the wolf.

Zol sighed. He knew it was just a matter of time. Tungo could not keep a secret; it was like trying to keep a cover on the boiling bag—eventually it boiled over.

They had removed the old bed of pine needles and were now hacking away with their axes at the mushy floor itself, digging down to the frozen part. They still had to scoop out all the smelly, melted mud and dump it. It was hard, dirty work, and they labored in heavy silence.

Tungo had brought two of the camp dogs to stand guard outside. Zol had tried, but he could not keep Koot from following him to the storage chamber. The crow sat on the roof—out of reach of the dogs—and teased them with raucous noises. It sounded like he was trying to imitate their barking, which made the dogs bark even more. Worse than that, he obviously enjoyed tormenting them.

Koot waited until the dogs were asleep. Then he would hop down and bravely strut between them. He would yank their tail hairs and peck at their shiny black toenails until he had them in a barking frenzy. When they snapped at him, he would do his crow laugh and fly away. Once he sat right on top of one dog's head and pecked him with his sharp beak until the dog was frantic and Zol himself was ready to wring Koot's neck!

Zol knew that the only thing keeping Tungo from killing Koot with pleasure was that everyone knew the crow belonged to Zol. One of the Star Dancers' sacred rules was that you never take or damage what belongs to someone else unless it is offered to you. If Tungo harmed Koot—unless he had a good reason—he would have to answer to Yakono.

Tungo's curiosity about Yakono's talk with Zol at the Balancing Rock finally got the best of him, and he broke the cold silence.

"Did Yakono tell you to get rid of that stupid crow?" he asked, not looking at Zol.

Zol did not answer at first, and the silence was filled by the barking, cawing din outside. "Yes," he said finally.

"Hah!" said Tungo. "I knew it! It's about time. What else did he say?" He sat back on his haunches and looked at Zol, eager to hear more.

Zol did not want to tell Tungo about his conversation with their leader. But he knew Tungo would not give up until Zol satisfied his curiosity.

"He talked to me about my father and about why we have the burning ceremony at Balancing Rock...do *you* know why?" Smoothly, Zol steered the conversation away from himself and to the meaning of Balancing Rock to the Star Dancers.

They worked in silence again until Zol said, "Maybe we should leave our mark someplace when we finish with this meat chamber—

you know, to show we were the ones to do such a good job cleaning it out."

"Oya!" Tungo's face lit up. "We could leave our handprints on the wall," he said eagerly. "I saw some by the entrance."

Tungo dug faster with his axe. "I know how to do it, too. You just chew on a piece of ochre until your mouth is full of spit. Then you put your hand against the wall and try to whistle at it." He laughed. "It gets all over everything except where your hand is. Come on, let's get this job done!"

Zol dug faster too, relieved that at least for now Tungo had forgotten about Koot. But Zol could not forget. He knew he had to obey Yakono and get rid of Koot. But *how*? How could he bear to part with his friend?

CHAPTER 17

WHY CROWS ARE BLACK

Zol sat on the flat rock outside his hotu and examined Tungo's crude spear-thrower. Koot waddled at his feet, looking for worms.

Zol's arms and shoulders still ached from working in the storage chamber. But now that it was finished, he had to think about replacing the spear-thrower he had lost to Tungo. He shook his head in disgust at the splintery piece of wood in his hands. He could not do anything with this. He decided to go and look for another chokecherry branch and try to make one like he had before.

At Zol's feet, Koot squawked in delight at finding a shiny green rock. He picked it up in his beak and flew off with it. Zol watched the bird with a heavy heart. He knew he could no longer put off obeying Yakono. While searching for the wood, he promised himself he would look for a family of crows for Koot to join.

The hotu flap opened, and Ona stepped out. She hobbled over to sit on a tree stump facing Zol. He noticed how stooped her shoulders were these days. She carried part of an elk leg bone and handed it to Zol.

"Will you crack this for me? I do not seem to be strong enough today."

Zol reached for his hammer and cracked it open easily. Handing it back, he saw that she had freshened the red ochre around her eyes and mouth.

"Ona, why do you keep painting your face with ochre?" he said irritably. "Nobody else in camp thinks crows are evil—except maybe Tungo. Even Yakono smiles at him."

"Pah! My brother knows better. Our mother knew the truth, and she tried to teach him like she taught me. But he was always off someplace with our father."

She pointed the leg bone at Zol and squinted her dark eyes. "My mother knew things the Star Dancers did not." Ona leaned forward as if telling him a big secret. "She was not really a Star Dancer, you know. They only found her after the Great Flood." She sat back with a smug look on her face.

"What?" Sometimes Zol wondered if Ona made up stories just to amuse herself. He knew, of course, about the Great Flood. But this was the first time he had ever heard *this* story! "Are you teasing me, Ona?"

Ona shook her head as she ran a fingernail along the thighbone, scooping out the pink marrow. "I would not tease my grandson about something so important." She put a piece of the soft marrow in her mouth and rolled it around with her tongue, savoring its rich flavor before she spoke again.

"That great wall of water came roaring down on the Star Dancers one day, like a monster. It picked up everything in its path—rocks, animals, people, huge trees and hunks of ice. Roaring, screaming and cracking, it swallowed them up. And when it was over, water covered all the land—hunting camps, hotus—everything. Only those people who were scouting or hunting high in the hills that day were spared.

"My own mother was swallowed up and carried by that icy monster. But then—by Earth's magic—she was spit out again, like a bitter berry. A Star Dancer found her caught in the branch of a pine tree—almost dead."

Ona leaned forward and spat out the next words. "And she was surrounded by black crows! Those screaming birds were just waiting for my poor mother to die. One evil bird was even pecking at her eyes. Oh, I cannot bear to think about it."

Koot picked the wrong time to squawk and fly back to Zol's shoulder. Zol quickly brushed him to the ground.

Ona narrowed her black eyes. "She was just a child, my mother...a child no older than Keena! The Star Dancers kept her as their own, but she was always different. Her beliefs were not like the others. Some say she was smarter. I do not know. I only know that she was my mother, and I believe what she told me."

Ona pointed at Koot. "Did you know that crows were once white?"

"Now I *know* you're just teasing me, Ona!"

"I am telling my grandson the truth," said Ona, holding her chin up like a stubborn child. "My mother knew.

"You can see for yourself how cocky is that crow of yours. He struts about like he owns this camp. Crows have always been like that."

She grunted. "Once they even flew to the man in the moon and sat on his shoulder. The people knew about it because the white crows came back carrying pieces of strange yellow rock in their bills—a kind never seen before."

Ona put another piece of marrow in her mouth and worked her wrinkled lips around it. "But that was not enough for those cocky crows," she continued. "Oh no. They decided to fly to Father Sun and sit on *his* shoulder! Can you imagine such disrespect?" She pinched her lips together.

"So how did they turn black?" asked Zol impatiently.

"They flew and they flew." Ona used her hands for effect, then pretended surprise. "Father Sun saw them coming and could not believe what he saw! He became angry and decided to teach those ungrateful birds a lesson."

Ona put her face close to Zol's. "Father Sun let those crows get close enough to him to be scorched black. Then he sent a strong wind to blow them crashing back to earth where they belonged...*and* he gave them a hunger for the flesh of dead things from that day forward!"

She sat up with a satisfied look on her face. "That is what happens to those who do not show proper respect to Father Sun."

Zol looked over at Koot, who had his sturdy legs braced while he tugged at a fat worm. The wind ruffled his feathers, causing little tufts to stick up on his back and head.

"Ona, look at Koot. How could this bird be evil?" At the mention of his name, the crow looked up. His black wings flashed blue and green in the sun. "Hello, Koot," said Zol, affectionately.

Koot gobbled the worm and flew over to land on Zol's arm. "Awwloo koot," repeated the crow, cocking his head to one side. He had begun imitating his favorite sounds.

Zol laughed, but Ona gasped and slapped her hand over her mouth. She jumped up and limped back to the hotu as fast as she could.

Before going inside, she turned and said, "See? A talking bird is a *sure* sign of evil. Get rid of him before it is too late!" She slipped inside and closed the flap tightly behind her.

"Come, Koot," said Zol, standing up. "It's time to find you a home where you'll be appreciated." He threw the crow into the air and started running.

CHAPTER 18

THE RED FOX

Zol found a group of chokecherry trees in a protected hollow near the river. He heard the river's roar, even though he could not see it. He began to look for a well-shaped branch from which he could carve a new spear-thrower. Koot waddled about in the tall grass, searching for crickets.

Zol's tool bag hung over his shoulder. The hafted spear points he called darts hung from his waist thong next to the short spears, and he carried Tungo's thrower. But he did not want to use it—even to practice. He laid it on the grass while he looked around.

Lost in his search for the perfect branch of chokecherry, Zol forgot about Koot, who had wandered off on his own. Koot often flew off by himself now, but not for long.

Finding a branch he thought would work, Zol took the stone axe from his tool bag and chopped the branch from the tree. Pleased with it, he twirled the wood in his hands and turned to call for Koot.

Zol's heart stopped. Instead of seeing Koot walking about with his funny head-thrusting walk, he saw a red fox pup slinking in the grass, its body slung low to the ground and tensing to pounce on something. Zol could not see Koot in the tall grass.

"Koot!" yelled Zol. But the wind was against him, and he knew his voice would not carry over the river noise. Zol ran toward the young fox, waving his arms to distract her. But it was too late. The red pup pounced and seized something black in her mouth and front paws.

"No!" shouted Zol, running as hard as he could. He dropped the piece of wood and grabbed his stone darts. The fox turned to lope into the trees with Koot in her mouth. Zol knew if he let her get to the trees, he would never find her again.

He pulled one of the sharp spear points back as far as he could and hurled it with all his might. It sailed over the fox's head. But she must have heard it because the young animal stopped and stared right at Zol. Koot struggled to get free from her mouth.

Zol's heart lurched as he pulled back another stone dart. He knew this was his last chance to save Koot. Taking a deep breath, he threw it with every bit of strength in his body.

The fox continued to stare at Zol in surprise as the spear point hit her right between the eyes and went into her skull. Her eyes opened wide and Koot fell from her mouth. The fox crumpled in a red heap.

When Zol reached Koot, the bird was no longer struggling. He lay there with his beak open, gasping for air, his eyes wild with fright. Zol scooped him up and pressed him against his cheek. He could feel the frightened little heart beating against his hand the way it had on the first day he had found him. A feeble "cu-koot" escaped his beak—so faint that Zol would never have heard it if the bird were not so close to his ear.

"Oh, Koot," he said, "please don't die." Tears dropped on the black feathers and rolled off as Zol felt all over the little body for wounds. Surprisingly, he found only two small holes from the fox's sharp fangs, and they were not bleeding badly. As he stroked Koot's head, back and wings, the bird began to relax and breathe normally. Only then did Zol look over at the dead fox.

Sympathy flooded through Zol for the beautiful red pup who was only doing what came naturally to her. She had to eat, too. But then the realization of what *he* had just done jolted him: not only had he saved Koot's life, he now had a red fox tail to hang from his waist— a sure sign of swiftness. Great Spirits!

He laid Koot gently in a clump of grass and took out his obsidian skinning blade. Working quickly, he sliced open the fox and removed the warm entrails. Then he removed the tail.

"Forgive me, sister fox," murmured Zol, as he worked. "But I could not let you kill my friend. I promise I will wear your tail proudly in honor of your swiftness."

The fox tail was reddish brown with a pure white tip. A thrill shot through Zol as he fastened it to his waist thong. He had not yet chosen a spirit sign; perhaps this was an omen. He stroked the fluffy tail.

"Wait until Tungo sees this, Koot!"

He slivered off some fresh fox meat and fed it to the crow. Koot swallowed greedily and opened his mouth for more. Zol laughed. "If you're that hungry, after what you've just been through, then you must be alright inside too."

Zol picked up the fox by its legs and slung it onto his shoulders. He could not wait to see Ona's face when he presented it to her. And the skin would make a perfect pillow fur for Keena.

A blood-curdling scream suddenly split the air right above him. Zol whirled around. A long-toothed cat crouched on the rock shelf above him! Its small ears were laid back and its powerful body twitched, preparing to pounce.

There was something odd about this cat: she only had one good fang. The other one was broken off in a jagged half tooth.

Zol remembered Tungo's spear-thrower lying in the grass where he had left it. It was no use to him now. He stared at the cat's fang— a long, curved slicing blade that would soon be stabbing into him if he did not do something fast! His heart hammered in his chest.

A low growl started in the back of the cat's throat and rose to a shrill scream. Zol's hands tightened around the fox's legs. He took a deep breath. The cat gathered her muscles and sprang from the ledge.

Zol threw the fox at her with every bit of strength he could summon. The carcass hit the cat in mid-air, and she screeched when it threw her off balance. She landed on top of the fox instead of Zol.

Then Zol saw how skinny and old she was. Long-toothed cats usually went after bigger game like bison—and even mammoth. But this cat was probably starving, because of her broken fang, and looking for anything at all. The smell of fox blood right under her nose diverted her attention from Zol. She growled and sank her teeth into the fox.

Zol did not stay to watch. He scooped up his crow from the grass and ran quickly back to camp. After he had placed Koot safely in Keena's care, Zol rushed over to Tungo's hotu to show him the fox tail. He could not wait to see Tungo's face when he told him about his encounter with the cat. For once *Zol* had something to brag about.

"I don't believe you," scoffed Tungo, after listening to Zol's story. "Who was with you?"

"Nobody," said Zol. "I was alone."

Tungo snorted. "I don't believe you," he repeated. "You were too scared to kill a wolf to save your own life, but now you're telling me that you were brave enough to kill a fox to save your stupid crow—and *then* face a long-toothed cat? ... Hah!

"Anyway, everyone knows that cats don't scream at the prey they are stalking!" Tungo scoffed, but his eyes kept darting to the fox tail hanging at Zol's waist.

"The cat wasn't after me," said Zol hotly. "She was stalking the fox! She screamed because I had what she wanted."

"I think you *found* that tail," said Tungo, narrowing his eyes. "You're not strong enough to kill an animal that size without a spear-thrower."

"Well, I did!" said Zol in a huff. He turned to leave.

"Wait!" said Tungo. He held out his hand. "Let me see the tail."

Proudly, Zol untied the foxtail and handed it to him. "It's a beauty, huh? See the pure white tip?"

"I could get one of these any time I wanted," boasted Tungo. "I just never wanted one."

But Zol noticed how Tungo kept running the shiny red tail through his cupped hand. Then two of the camp dogs started snapping viciously at each other, and Tungo thrust the foxtail back at Zol.

"I have to take care of my dogs," he said, turning away. But Zol had seen the spark of envy in Tungo's eyes.

CHAPTER 19

TEACHING TUNGO

"I cannot make fox stew from a tail," said Ona. "Next time act like a hunter...use your *spears* to kill the cat and bring the fox home to me!"

But her words could not hide the sparkle of pride and excitement in her eyes when she listened to Zol's cat story. She had not even argued when he told her he wanted to wait until Koot's wounds healed before finding a crow family for him.

Tungo had insisted that Zol show him where the long-toothed cat had attacked him. So Zol took Tungo to the grassy spot below the rocky ledge. Clumps of reddish hair and pieces of entrails made it obvious that the fox had indeed been eaten there, but Tungo still wasn't convinced it was a long-toothed cat. While he looked for tracks, Zol retrieved Tungo's spear-thrower and found the piece of chokecherry he had dropped while running after the fox. He left Tungo searching for cat tracks and returned to camp.

Back at camp, Zol bent to the task of resharpening his long carnelian blade. It had become dull from carving out the rough shape of his new spear-thrower, and Zol liked to keep his tools sharp. Using an antler tip, he pressed off little reddish flakes from one side of the blade and then the other, making a sharp new edge.

Koot hopped back and forth from Zol's shoulder to his knee, and then to the ground to inspect the shiny stone flakes. He liked to pick them up and move them around with his beak.

The days were long and warm now. The wind blew almost constantly, which was good, because it kept the biting insects from being unbearable. And it helped the Star Dancers with their work.

In front of every hotu, racks of split-open fish and thin strips of meat were drying in the sun and wind. The people were busy from dawn to dusk, taking advantage of these long summer days to gather and prepare food for the winter, when the roots, nuts, and berries that Mother Earth gave them so generously in the warm days would be buried under deep snow. Their winter camp protected them from the harsh weather, but it did not give them abundant food.

Keena sat cross-legged on the ground next to a pile of yellow-green willow shoots she and Mother had cut. She was trying to make a collecting basket by herself the way Mother had taught her. She concentrated so hard, the tip of her tongue stuck out at the side of her mouth.

It tickled Zol to see her so intent on her work. The crystal bird pendant he had made for her swung from her neck as she bent over. It sparkled in the sunlight, shooting out colors of the rainbow.

Koot liked that shiny crystal almost as much as Ona's amber piece. He spotted it now and screeched with delight. He ran over to Keena, his tail waggling from side to side as he ran. Zol laughed.

"Watch out, Keena! Koot has seen your bird pendant."

Keena's hand quickly flew to the sparkling stone and tucked it inside her tunic. "Oh no you don't," she said to Koot. She ran her small hand lovingly over the sleek black crow, then returned to her willow weaving.

But Koot found that interesting, too, and started to pull at the shaggy ends that were sticking out.

"Get away, Koot!" said Keena, pushing him aside. She was having trouble keeping all the slippery stems together, and her patience was wearing thin. But when she looked up again, her frown turned to a happy grin. "Ho, Tungo!"

Tungo stood behind Zol. His stout, brown body was bare to the waist, and his strong arms were folded across his chest. He frowned at Koot.

Koot squawked and made little threatening dashes toward Tungo.

"Koot, come!" ordered Zol. Obediently, Koot flew over to Zol's knee. "Koot-kom," mimicked the crow.

Tungo's eyes widened in surprise at the crow's imitation of Zol. Then they narrowed again, and his face was sullen as he said, "Yakono told me I had to come here and watch you chip stones." He looked down and scuffed the dirt with his toes. "He said I have to learn to make better points." He looked at Zol miserably.

Zol knew how hard this was for Tungo. He had avoided Zol's hotu for almost a full moon—ever since Koot had humiliated him in front of everyone. It was obvious he did not want to be here today. But a Star Dancer did not disobey his leader.

Ona, who had been pounding dried fish with a mallet, looked up. "He is a wise man, my brother," she said. "It is not good to have bad feelings between you two. You have played together like brothers since you were babies."

Zol knew that Ona had missed Tungo's visits; and so had Keena. She sat there smiling, with obvious affection in her warm, brown eyes. Zol also noticed that the rabbit-fur pouch she had worked so hard on now hung at Tungo's waist.

Tungo glared at Koot. "Just keep your evil bird away from me, oya?"

As if he knew he was being talked about, Koot screeched again from Zol's knee. Zol carried him over to his roosting tree and threw him toward the branches. "Stay there, Koot," Zol ordered.

Koot did not disappear up to his roost, but stayed on the long branch that reached out toward the hotu. He walked back and forth, stopping every now and then to glare and screech at Tungo.

Before long, Tungo's first discomfort at being forced to come wore off and he was his old bragging self, boasting to Ona and Keena about his latest hunting successes. The women fawned over him as if he were the greatest hunter in the clan.

But Zol had to admit that for once Tungo really seemed interested in making better stone points. Tungo watched carefully as Zol showed him how to press in and down at the same time, with his pressure tool, to send long thin flakes across the stone point in a regular pattern. Tungo's short, fat fingers made the finishing details harder for him, but he tried. He asked questions and actually listened to Zol's answers.

"Let me show you a trick Mother taught me," said Zol, reaching for Tungo's point. "When the point is almost done, you chip out a little groove at the base and run it up toward the tip."

Tungo quickly pulled his point away. "Play tricks with your own points, Zol. I worked hard on this one."

"It's not that kind of a trick," said Zol. "Look." He held up one of his own finished points. "See how I chipped a groove on both sides so that it is thinner at the bottom?" He pulled out one of his hafted spear tips. "See? It fits better into the shaft that way, and it doesn't wobble so much when the spear hits the target."

Tungo looked at Zol's spear tip. The straight willow shaft was carved to a point at one end, and the other end held a slender green stone point, tightly bound to the shaft with sinew and glued with pine sap.

"Here, try to wiggle it loose," offered Zol.

Tungo grabbed it and tried to force it loose, cutting his hand. "Owk!" He dropped the spear and sucked at his hand.

"See? It won't wobble loose when you thrust it into an animal either," said Zol.

Before Father Sun had disappeared behind the mountains, Tungo had made two decent-looking dart tips and one long, carnelian knife blade like Zol's. He was so pleased with himself that when Koot woke up from his nap in the tree and started screeching at him, he just ignored it. He sat next to Keena to show her his knife blade.

Ona looked up from her work. "Have you not finished that basket yet, child?" she asked Keena in irritation.

"Almost," said Keena. She held it up for all to see. Tungo praised it, but Zol thought it looked like the nest he had tried to weave for Koot. Pieces of willow stuck out in every direction. It was *almost* round, though, and Keena had even made a flat, round cover for it.

"Good," said Ona in approval. "Tomorrow morning I want you to test it by collecting crickets for me."

"Oya!" exclaimed Keena, grinning and clapping.

Zol was not sure what Keena liked best—catching the crickets or eating them. Every summer, if the children caught crickets for her, Ona would steam them in layers of grass in the fire pit. Then she would set them out to dry in the sun until they were crispy and chewy. It was Ona's special delicacy—and the family's favorite snack. Ona sometimes used them to barter for things she wanted.

"Tungo, will you come with us?" asked Keena, shyly.

"Good idea," said Ona. "More hands make for faster picking. Remember, though, you have to get them early in the morning while they are still numb from the cold."

A wide grin split Tungo's face, deepening his dimples. "I'll be here for the morning greeting," he said.

Zol groaned silently.

CHAPTER 20

WOMAN ON THE MOUNTAIN

True to his word, Tungo was there before Father Sun had peeked over the ridge. After the morning greeting, the children chewed on strips of cold elk meat and drank hot dandelion broth. Then Ona gave them pemmican and root cakes to take with them in a soft carrying pouch. She asked Keena to fill the pouch with camas bulbs and onions on the way back.

Father Sun was still low in the sky when the three set out toward the river, and their long shadows danced ahead of them. Koot flew along with them, making a whooshing sound over their heads. Then he seemed to remember that Tungo was his enemy and dove at the boy's tangled mass of black hair. He pecked him hard with his sharp beak and flew away.

"Owk! Stop it!" Tungo flailed helplessly at Koot with his arms.

"If your hair didn't look so much like a crow's nest, maybe he'd leave you alone," said Zol, laughing.

Tungo looked embarrassed and glanced at Keena. "That bird just hates me, that's all," he whined.

Tungo was so intent on watching out for Koot that he kept stumbling over rocks in the path. Keena giggled. Tungo's eyes sparkled. He started tripping deliberately until he fell flat on his face. Keena laughed out loud.

"I know what," said Tungo. "Keena, let me have your basket. He took off the cover and turned it upside down over his head. "There," he said, his voice muffled inside the basket, "now that stupid crow can peck at me all he wants." He had no sooner finished speaking, when he walked off the path and right into a tree.

Keena clapped her hands and laughed so hard tears came to her eyes.

Soon they found a cluster of bushes loaded with crickets. They got right to work picking the crickets—like hard dark berries—off the bushes. It had been a cold night, and the insects were still numb from the cold.

"Ona was right," said Keena. "Catching crickets like this is a lot easier than chasing after them when they're warmed up."

"But not as much fun," Tungo said. "I like it better when they're hopping all over the place."

When Keena's basket was crammed full of crickets, she tightly tied on the cover. Then they sat on a rocky ledge overlooking the river to eat the meal they had brought.

"Look," said Keena, pointing to the mountains. "You can see the Woman On The Mountain from here."

Zol had seen it before, but he marveled again at the way the mountain ridge formed an almost perfect profile of a woman lying on her back. Her face, breasts and toes pointed toward the sky. Her hair, arms, and tunic flowed gracefully down the mountainside.

"I never saw that before," said Tungo, his eyes round with surprise.

"Ona told me that if it weren't for the Woman On The Mountain, none of us would be here," said Keena.

Tungo scoffed. "If it weren't for Yakono, you mean. I never heard of a woman leading the Star Dancers."

"No," said Keena, "she wasn't a leader. Her name was Makura. Everyone thought she was strange because she would get up by herself every morning before dawn, raise her hands to the east, and sing to Father Sun as he came over the hills."

"That isn't strange," said Tungo.

"Not now," said Keena, "but it was then. And she used to go off by herself and be gone for days. People said that she talked to the animals...and that the animals understood her!"

Tungo raised his eyebrows at Zol. "That *is* odd," he said. "Especially if she talked to birds!"

Zol looked at Koot. The crow had stretched out his wings in a shiny black arc on one of the rocks to soak up the sunshine. "Maybe she came from another clan, like Ona's mother," he suggested.

Tungo frowned. "Go on, Keena."

"One day Father Sun went down behind those mountains like he always does," said Keena, pointing to the Woman On The Mountain. "Only the next day he did not come up again.

...or the day after that." Her eyes got big. "There were no stars at night...and no moon either."

The way Keena told her story in a singsong voice, she sounded just like Ona, thought Zol in amusement.

Tungo shivered. "Sacred Mammoth! It must have been cold!"

Keena nodded. "The people huddled together in one big shelter and kept a fire going; but the earth got colder and colder. Ice grew over the camp. They could not hunt or fish, and the food was running out.

"Makura said to them, 'See? Father Sun is angry at your disrespect. He wants the children of the earth to greet him every morning at dawn like the birds in the trees and the crickets in the grass. Father Sun wants his children to sing to him.'

"But the people turned on her. They became angry and blamed Makura for Father Sun's disappearance. They sent her away all by herself."

Keena sighed.

"Well, don't stop now," pleaded Tungo. "What happened?"

"The people sent her away to find Father Sun and beg his forgiveness for them. They all watched as she left the shelter and walked toward the mountains. She got smaller and smaller...and then disappeared from their sight. She never returned."

The three ate their meal in silence and stared at the Woman On The Mountain. Finally, Keena continued.

"The people started dying one by one. The strongest ones kept the fire going and melted water to drink. Then one day, when those that were still alive had given up hope, Father Sun peeked over the mountain and rose into the sky."

Tungo let out his breath in a gush, as if he had been holding it.

"Even though they were weak, the people danced with joy and sang in the warmth of that day. And at night one bright star—brighter than all the rest—hung over the mountain.

"The people danced all night, too, under the light of that star, so they could be sure to greet Father Sun when he appeared the next morning." Keena looked intently at Tungo to make sure he understood.

"See, they believed that Makura had *found* Father Sun and convinced him to return. That is why we greet Father Sun every morning—the way she taught us—and why we are called Star Dancers."

"But why did Makura turn to stone?" asked Tungo.

"She didn't turn to stone," said Keena. "After Father Sun returned, the people saw the Woman On The Mountain for the first time. They knew it was a sign: Makura had died saving them, and her spirit became a star to watch over them."

Zol looked over at Koot, who had finished sunning himself and was now preening his black feathers. If this story were true, could Ona's story about crows flying to the moon be true?

CHAPTER 21

THE RIVER BECKONS

The three children stared in silence at the Woman on the Mountain, letting the story sink in. As they watched, dark clouds bunched together in the sky and rolled toward them like huge balls of grey fur. They heard the low rumble of thunder in the distance.

"Oh!" said Keena. "I'd better find the onions and bulbs for Ona before it starts to rain."

Zol jumped up. "While you do that, I'm going to scout for rocks down by the river. Mother never looks there."

"No, Zol!" said Keena, her eyes big with concern. "Look at the way the river tosses those trees around as if they were pieces of bark." She shivered. "It's too dangerous, Zol, and Mother told us to stay away."

"I won't go too close," he assured her.

Tungo puffed up. "I'd better stay here with Keena and protect her," he said. "My brother said he saw cat prints around here a few days ago, and for me to watch out for it." He fingered the cat tooth on his neck thong, which now had a wolf fang on either side of it.

"I'll be a lookout for Keena while she digs. But take your bird with you." He glared at Koot, who had suddenly become fascinated with Tungo's collection of teeth and cocked his head to stare at them.

"Koot, come!" said Zol quickly. Koot flew to his shoulder, but kept staring at Tungo's neck and stepped back and forth restlessly. Zol put his hand over him. "I won't be long," he said. "I'll meet you back here." With his hand still on Koot, Zol ran down the hill toward the river.

"I should be the one protecting my sister," he said to Koot, "not Tungo." But he had to admit that she was probably safer with Tungo.

Released from Zol's hand, Koot flew on ahead, attracted by a tree full of raucous black crows. Zol stopped and watched him, happy that he was showing some interest in the other crows.

In the past, Koot would look up when crows flew over, but had never shown any interest in flying with them. "Go ahead, Koot," said Zol softly. "Now is the perfect time."

But Koot lost interest in the crows because something else had captured his attention. He was dancing back and forth on a fallen tree that jutted out over the edge of the steep river bank.

Zol did not like to get too close to the edge. He had heard stories about people who were swallowed up by this violent river when the ground beneath them crumbled away. But now his curiosity overcame his fear.

Koot was pacing and screeching at something in the water. Zol could barely hear the crow over the fierce roar of the river, but he could tell how excited Koot was from the way he jabbed his head forward with every "sqraawwk!"

Zol crept closer on his hands and knees. Hanging onto the tree, he peered over the edge. The crashing waters sent a fine cold spray up into his face. Then he saw it: A piece of clear crystal as big as his hand lay just out of reach of the water. Caught in the crook of a tree branch, and washed with spray, it sparkled in the sunlight with more colors than Zol knew existed. He sucked in his breath. Great Spirits! It was beautiful!

Koot thought so, too. He paced back and forth making little hops and spreading his wings as if to fly, but then changing his mind. Zol realized that Koot, too, must have a healthy respect for this river, or he would have pounced on that shiny stone without hesitation.

The crystal rocked back and forth. Zol knew that in a very short time it would be swept away with all the other debris in the river. If he could reach that crystal before it disappeared, just think of the beautiful pendant he could make for Mother! He imagined her face lighting up as he presented her with a finely-chipped stone to wear on a thong around her neck. That made up his mind; he had to have it!

Farther down the bank he saw a young willow tree that had fallen over when most of its roots were undermined by water. Its long green tendrils bounced and floated on the water, but some of the roots were still attached to the bank. If he could climb down that tree to the water's edge, he might be able to reach the crystal rock.

Zol slipped off his tool bag and tunic to make himself lighter. He removed his waist thong, with his darts and fox tail, and laid them on top of the tunic. Then he tugged at the willow to test it; it seemed sturdy enough to hold him. With his back to the river, he straddled the tree and started easing himself down.

The trunk was about as big around as his leg and more slippery than he thought it would be. He dug his toes into the crumbly gravel of the bank as he worked his way down. The freezing water sprayed his back and took his breath away. Father Sun slipped behind the dark rolling clouds. A loud clap of thunder bellowed overhead, startling Zol so that he almost lost his hold. Koot flew in circles around him, screeching in excitement.

Zol's heart hammered in his chest; the roaring filled his head. He was afraid to look behind him at the raging water. He forced himself to concentrate on that crystal rock and his mother's face. When he got down as far as he could, he looked over at the crystal. It was even more beautiful up close—it beckoned to him.

He forgot his fear and wrapped his left arm around the small tree trunk. Hanging on tightly, he reached out with his right arm toward the sparkling rock. He could almost touch it, but not quite. He needed to be about a foot-length closer...then it would be his.

Digging his feet farther into the slippery soil, Zol leaned back and tried to pull the tip of the willow over to the right. It moved a little, but not enough. He gave it another yank. Suddenly, the remaining roots gave way on the bank, sending a shower of stones down on Zol. He felt the whole tree moving down toward the river. He let go of the tree and lunged for the side of the steep bank, clawing at some wet rocks that jutted out. As he did, his foot kicked the crystal rock—dislodging it—and he saw it bounce into the river, disappearing into the froth. He froze.

Somehow his hand and foot-holds kept him balanced there, but he was afraid to move. He was sure that if he did, he would disappear like that crystal into the froth and never be seen again. The boulders cracking together in the water sounded like jaws waiting to snap him up if he let go. The roar of the river came at him from all sides, and thunder growled overhead—like giant, long-toothed cats waiting to devour him.

"Help!" he screamed into the roar. He knew nobody could hear him. If he did not climb away from there soon, he would be torn away and swallowed by the river. But he could not move! Oh, *why* had he not listened to Keena?

CHAPTER 22
TUNGO TO THE RESCUE

Zol's eyes were clenched shut when he felt sharp claws dig into his bare arm. He opened his eyes to see Koot frantically scolding him. "Koot!" Relief flooded through Zol until he realized that a bird—even one as smart as Koot—could not help him. Or could he?

"Go get Tungo, Koot!" he shouted above the noise. "Tungo!"

"Kawk! Kawk! Kawk!" screamed Koot into Zol's ear. He flew in circles over Zol's head and then flew away.

Zol felt the first big drops of rain land on his back. Surprisingly, they felt warm and comforting. He thought of his mother and her beautiful face. He imagined her eyes, deep green pools, when Keena told her that her only son had been swept away by the river. A lump formed in his throat, and a sob escaped. No! He would not let that sadness happen to her again. He must try!

He stepped up with his right foot, but the loose gravel gave way under it, and he slid down even farther, grasping frantically for new handholds. He pressed his face against the cold bank and cried.

A picture of Balancing Rock flashed in Zol's head and Yakono's voice echoed: "When it is our time to die, we die...it is nothing to fear." But he *was* afraid! He was shivering so much it took all his strength to hang on. The rain came steadily now.

Zol felt himself slipping. He looked up, desperate for something—anything—to grab onto. A thick willow root stuck out of the bank more than an arm-length above his head. Should he lunge for it? Would it hold him if he reached it? The hungry river ate away at the bank under his feet; boulders cracked together as they raced by—waiting to smash him. He had no choice.

With a giant push, Zol screamed and lunged for the exposed root. His right hand closed around it. He dangled wildly over the river from one arm until he found footholds and could grab it with both hands. Clinging to the root, he felt more secure. But for how long? There was nothing else within reach above him. Was this it, then? Zol closed his eyes, exhausted.

He thought he was dreaming when he felt something soft and scratchy move against his face. He opened his eyes and saw a willow rope dangling in front of him. He looked up to see Keena's round face next to Tungo's staring down at him with terrified eyes.

"Grab onto the rope," shouted Tungo, "and walk up the bank. I'll hold on to this end."

"I can't!" screamed Zol. "I can't move or I'll fall into the river!"

Then he felt Koot's sharp claws again, digging into his arm. "Kawk! Kawk!" he screeched. The crow grasped the swinging green rope in his beak and ran up Zol's arm, dropping it on his hands.

Gathering his courage, Zol tried to loosen his cramped fingers from their death grip on the root. Koot stood on his arm, pecking at the braided willow rope. "Kawk! Kawk!" he screamed relentlessly.

Zol opened one hand and grabbed for the rope. But before his stiff fingers could clasp it, the rope swung away from him. He felt his left foot slipping. He pressed himself even harder against the bank.

"Try again!" Tungo shouted over the river noise.

This time Zol was able to grasp it and hang on, but his right foot slipped. He unclenched his other hand and grabbed onto the rope with both hands just as both footholds crumbled away beneath him.

Swinging clumsily back and forth, he scrambled with his feet, trying to catch hold of one of the slippery rocks that jutted out. The rope felt secure in his hands and gave Zol confidence. Raindrops pelted his bare skin, but he hardly felt them. He walked up the bank using Tungo's sturdy body like a tree trunk for support.

At the top, he collapsed in a muddy heap and broke into sobs of relief. Keena was crying, too, and her dripping hair stuck to her face as she tried to help him into his tunic.

———

Back in camp, dry and warm again, their hands wrapped around cups of sage tea, the children told Mother and Ona about Zol's narrow escape.

"Aaiiee!" shrieked Ona, clapping a bony hand over her mouth. "See, it is starting already. That evil bird lured Zol over the edge to get him swallowed up by the river."

"No!" protested Keena. "Koot *saved* him. We were waiting for Zol, when Koot came back without him and screeched at Tungo. At first we thought he was after Tungo's cat tooth, and we tried to shoo him away. But then he started saying 'koot come, koot come'—like he does when he imitates Zol. He kept flying away and coming back. We followed him and that's how we found Zol's tool bag and tunic by the river's edge."

Tungo agreed with Keena and nodded. "It's true, Ona," he said. "And when Keena braided a willow rope to lower over the edge, Zol could not have caught it without Koot's help." He shook his head in disgust. "He was scared stiff again—just like that time he startled the wolf with its kill. I had to save him that time, too, remember?"

Zol glared at Tungo, and Tungo slapped his hand over his mouth. "Ooops!" He looked guilty, but Zol thought he saw a triumphant glint in his eyes.

Ona's eyes widened. "That was just after he brought that bad-luck crow to camp—aaiiee!" She wrapped her thin arms around her body and swayed back and forth, moaning softly.

"But you said that you never even *saw* the wolf until Tungo killed it," said Keena, looking puzzled.

Mother looked at him with surprise, and Zol saw disappointment in her eyes. At that moment, Zol almost wished he had let go of the tree root and been swept away.

A Star Dancer faced dangers every day that required bravery. Where Zol's courage should be, was there just a black hole? Great Spirits! Would it not be better to go through life with only one arm than to be a Star Dancer without courage?

CHAPTER 23
MOTHER'S GIFT

The following days were miserable ones for Zol. He developed a bad cold and dragged himself around camp in a mean mood. He snapped at Keena and refused the cough remedy that Ona had prepared for him from mullein roots. When Mother talked to him about some new rocks she had found, he showed no interest.

Ona had steamed all the crickets in Keena's basket and laid them out carefully on strips of birch bark so they could dry thoroughly in the sun and wind. It was too much temptation for Koot; he loved those crunchy crickets! Ona kept an eye on him while she worked— and a long willow switch in her hand. She took great pleasure in snapping it at Koot when he tried to steal a cricket.

But even Koot's antics did not cheer Zol. He sat on his flat rock working halfheartedly on the new spear-thrower. It was not turning out as well as his first one, and Zol was losing patience.

The weather did not help; it was hot and muggy. Distant rumbles of thunder sounded like herds of bison running, but rain did not come to clear the heavy air. Zol slapped angrily at the biting flies that attacked his bare skin, leaving red, itchy welts. But it was too hot to wear pants and tunic for protection.

Keena sat in the shade of a pine tree blowing a tune on the bird-bone whistle that Zol had made for her. Usually Zol loved to hear her play, but today the high clear notes grated on his nerves.

"Keena, do you have to do that now?" he snapped. "I'm trying to concentrate."

Mother looked at Zol. "Why are you frowning so, Zol?"

Abruptly, Zol looked up and threw his unfinished spear-thrower as far as he could. "This is terrible!" he said. "Why did I ever let Tungo have my good one? I'll never be able to make another one as good as that." He knew he was whining, but he could not help it. His head ached and his nose was plugged up.

"I'm supposed to be practicing for the mammoth hunt, and I don't even have a thrower to practice with." He started coughing and could not stop.

Mother got a cup of the cough potion that Ona had prepared and brought it to him. He shoved it away. Mother gently insisted, and Zol finally took a big swallow. The bitter drink made him gag.

Mother squatted in front of him and held both his hands in hers. "I think I have something that will make you feel better," she said. Her large green eyes held his. Tiny gold flecks in the green reminded Zol of the calm lake at evening, and he felt cooler just looking at her.

Mother stood up and went inside the hotu. When she came back, she carried something wrapped in a soft, speckled fawn skin. She laid it on his lap. "I have been saving this for you," she said, her eyes glowing. "I thought I would give it to you just before the mammoth hunt, but I think now is a better time."

Zol slowly unwrapped the heavy object and sucked in his breath. What he held in his hands was the most beautiful spear-thrower he had ever seen. Even Yakono's could not compare with it.

It was carved in a simple design from mammoth tusk and polished to a sheen from use.

Zol could not speak. His mouth fell open, and his eyes questioned Mother. She smiled at him, obviously pleased with his reaction to her gift. "I made this for your father when he asked me to start a hotu with him. He always told me it was my spear-thrower, not his arm, that made him such a good hunter." Her eyes sparkled. "Of course that was not true, but I loved to hear it anyway."

"But...but," sputtered Zol, "it's too...it's too..." His eyes filled with tears, and he blurted out, "Mother, I'm not worthy of my father's spear-thrower!" He started to wrap it up and hand it back to her, but she stopped him with her hands and looked deep into his eyes.

"You are your father's son, Zol, and I am very proud of you. I will always be proud of you. This is yours. It always has been." She got up and went back into the hotu.

Zol sat there stunned, turning the beautiful piece over in his hands. A crosshatch pattern was carved in the base of the hand grip and repeated along the slender shaft. On the top sat a carved loon—Mother's spirit sign—with its sharp bill turned down to hold the spear.

He tossed it gently into the air and caught it, to get the feel and weight of it. To think that his own father's hands had used this very tool to hurl spears at the mammoth!

Zol wanted to be alone with his amazing gift, so he took the water bags to the lake. The water was calm and clear, like Mother's eyes, and the air felt cooler. Zol held the spear-thrower and looked across the lake at the sacred mammoth sign.

Summer had turned the grassy hills around it to the rich yellow color of bear fat. And because the mammoth shape was lava rock, it stood out in greater contrast now than it had in the spring. The birch trees that formed the mammoth's tusks were beginning to turn. Zol knew that when the tusks turned bright red, it would be time to hunt the mammoth. He squeezed the piece of mammoth tusk in his hands. It would not be long now.

Cross-legged, he sat on the shore of the lake for a long time, holding Father's spear-thrower. An idea was forming in his mind...an idea that would prove once and for all if he did indeed have his father's courage.

CHAPTER 24

MARK OF THE MAMMOTH

The Star Dancers circled in dream motion and pointed at Zol. "Your father's son...your father's son," they chanted.

Then the pointing arms became brown hairy trunks, and Zol was surrounded by mammoths. They raised their trunks and trumpeted shrilly. He turned to run, but his feet were tangled in berry vines and he fell flat on his face.

Then the trumpeting became laughter. Zol looked over his shoulder and saw the Star Dancers again. They were pointing at him and laughing.

The laughter filled his head. Zol clamped his hands over his ears and shouted, "Stop it!"

———————

Zol woke up in a sweat. He lay in the dark hotu, thinking about the dream until his heartbeat returned to normal. Then he picked up father's spear-thrower and squeezed it. He would do it now, before he changed his mind. He could no longer live with the fear that gnawed at his insides like a rat.

He crept quietly out of the hotu without waking anyone. It had cooled during the night and a blanket of fog hung over Mammoth Camp. In the dimness, the other shelters looked like large hairy animals hunkered down for the night. Zol shivered and glanced at Koot's roosting tree. He did not want the crow to follow him this time.

Silently, he trotted out of camp and toward the hills. Zol touched the elkskin pouch at his waist in which he carried a horn cup of powdered red ochre mixed with fat. He carried Father's spear-thrower to give him courage. And the soft touch of the fox tail brushing against his leg as he ran gave him comfort.

Running in long strides over the damp grass, Zol felt his fears disappearing like fog in the morning sun. Yakono was right. Why should he fear Mother Mammoth? She gave the Star Dancers her meat for the long winters when they could not hunt. She gave them her thick hide to cover their hotus and protect them from snow and rain. She even gave them her bones for tools. She gave them life.

Zol stopped to catch his breath and observe the morning greeting. Then he pulled a dried berry cake from his pouch and bit into it to quiet his growling stomach. Father Sun had burned away the fog, and Zol inhaled the sweet scent of sage. He looked around him. To the west, the mountains of ice that never melted glowed amber in the early-morning light. But Zol was running east toward Father Sun and the great wall of melting ice.

Suddenly a bellowing scream pierced the morning calm. Zol's heart jumped to his throat. A mammoth! The berry cake became like dried bunchgrass in his mouth, and he could not swallow it. His heart pounded.

He could still change his mind and go back. Nobody knew what he was doing. He would say he had gone out early to search for chipping rocks.

But something made him go forward instead, toward the sound. The men in his clan faced death every day; they did not run away from it. To be a Star Dancer *meant* to have courage.

He saw them on the next hill. The herd of mammoths moved slowly along a wide stream bordered by slender willows and birches. They browsed on sedges and young willow trees as they went. Zol stopped to watch them. He swallowed hard. They were giants!

The shaggy brown creatures moved on legs like tree trunks. They were so tall that a Star Dancer could easily run under one without touching its belly. And the tusks!

Zol's own legs felt weak. What he came to do suddenly seemed impossible—like sprouting wings and flying over the tree tops. He shook his head. He could not do it; he could not mark the mammoth like his father had.

But what if he just went closer and watched from a safe distance? Then he could report back to Yakono, like a scout. Zol moved forward.

At the stream, he crouched low and moved silently toward the herd as he had been taught. He knew mammoths had poor eyesight, but very good hearing, so he stayed in the trees, close to the water. He remembered to stay downwind so they could not smell him.

A crunching, grinding noise close to him made Zol freeze. The willow tree next to him shook and bent over. Zol's heart hammered against his chest, but he remained perfectly still—like a quail in the underbrush. A *mammoth* stood on the other side of the trees!

The brown mountain of hair moved downstream into a clear spot. Zol saw that it was a young mammoth that had strayed away from the herd. She spotted Zol and stopped chewing. She pointed her trunk at him as if trying to smell him.

Do not run! Zol told himself. Do not run!

Willow leaves stuck out the sides of the mammoth's mouth. Dark beady eyes, set low on her head, watched Zol. Her small ears flicked back and forth, as if trying to hear this strange creature. Zol noticed a big notch in one of her ears, as if it had once been torn badly. She

did not seem alarmed, just curious. She began to chew again, slowly grinding up the fresh willow shoots in her giant teeth.

A cold chill snaked down Zol's back. The mammoth was close enough to reach out and grab him with her long trunk. He stared at the pointed tusks that curved out at him like monstrous fangs.

She took a step toward Zol, stretching her hairy trunk out at him. Zol closed his eyes and held his breath—waiting. Something touched his hair. A tingle zapped through Zol's body like lightning. Then he felt a blast of her warm, smelly breath on his face.

A blaring cry split the air so suddenly that Zol screamed. He clapped his hand over his mouth, wild-eyed with fear. But the young mammoth only tossed her head, trumpeted an answering call and lumbered away to follow the herd.

Zol collapsed like a skin without bones. He crawled to the stream and splashed the cold water on his face. Drinking from his cupped hands, he felt the sun's warmth on his back.

"I did not touch the mammoth," he said to the chuckling stream, "but the great mammoth touched *me*." A smile of wonder stretched across Zol's face. "And I did not run away!"

Father Sun's warmth spread to his insides. Zol turned away from the stream and trotted back to Mammoth Camp.

CHAPTER 25

TUNGO'S SCATTER TOOL

Zol pulled off his hide tunic and carried it as he trotted over the yellow grassland. It was going to be another hot day.

Before he saw Mammoth Camp, Zol saw a single black crow circling high in the pale blue sky. He cupped his hands and called, "Caw! Caw!" in perfect imitation of Koot.

"Caw! Caw!" answered Koot, flying straight for Zol.

As usual, Zol's heart filled with gladness when he watched that wild bird spiral out of the sky and land on his shoulder. "Hello, Koot," he said, running his hand over the sleek bird. He broke off a piece of his half-eaten berry cake and gave it to the crow. Then he brought Koot around to face him.

"I saw the mammoth today, Koot, and the mammoth saw me." He stroked the crow's black beak. "In fact, Koot, the mammoth *touched* me. And I did not run away!"

Koot gurgled and opened his beak for more berry cake. "Awwloo koot," he said. Zol laughed and gave him another piece.

"It is a good omen, Koot. But I can't tell anybody ...not yet."

Zol placed Koot back on his shoulder and continued trotting back to camp. Keena ran to meet him. "Where were you, Zol? We were all worried about you."

"I had something important to do," he said.

Koot hopped to Keena's head and started preening the short hairs on her forehead. She pushed him away, and he flew off with a "squawk."

"There you are, Zol," said Mother, coming up behind Keena. "Where did you go off to so early?"

"I wanted to go by myself to try Father's spear-thrower for the first time," said Zol. He did not lie. On his way back to camp, he had stopped to make a target and practice with the thrower.

"You know what will happen when Tungo sees it." Zol ran his fingers lightly over the carved loon and looked directly into Mother's eyes.

"Mother, this is truly amazing," he said, raising the spear-thrower with both hands. "It is like an extension of my own arm. I made heart-hit after heart-hit with it." He grinned. "I could not make a thrower as good as this if I lived forever. I think Father was right about it; it was the spear-thrower, not me, that hit the mark.

Then Zol did something he had not done since he was a little boy: he grabbed his mother and hugged her. "Thank you, Mother!"

Mother's grin matched Zol's as she hugged him back. Then she held him at arm's length and said, "Zol, I have been dreaming of this day for years."

Tungo always seemed to know when something was going on at their hotu, and he trotted into camp now. "Ho, Zol," he said. "What is that you're holding?"

"Ho, Tungo," said Zol. "Look what Mother gave me." He held it out for Tungo's inspection. "It's my father's spear-thrower."

Tungo's eyes got big, and he almost drooled on it. "Yazoo, what a beauty!" He ran his dirt-stained fingers over the mammoth ivory reverently and gave a low whistle. Without looking up, he said, "Can I try it?"

Then he looked at Zol. "I came to tell you that Yakono says you have to go hunting with me today, so that I can show you some tricks."

"That is true, Zol," said Mother. "Yakono was here right after the morning greeting to talk to you, but you were gone."

Koot spotted Tungo and flew toward the boys, screeching. He landed on Zol's head and scolded Tungo noisily, stepping back and forth from one foot to the other. Even though Tungo now tolerated the crow, Koot had obviously not forgotten the time Tungo slapped him to the ground.

Tungo frowned. "Leave your crow here," he said, "or I won't go— and then you'll have to answer to Yakono."

"Keena, will you keep Koot here?" asked Zol. He handed the crow to his sister, and she took him inside the hotu.

"Wait until I eat something," said Zol, "and then I'll go with you. You won't believe how well Father's spear-thrower works until you try it yourself."

Mother grinned at Zol as she handed him a bowl of rabbit stew and a dried root cake.

Tungo still held the spear-thrower. His eyes were full of envy as he stroked it and turned it over in his hands. "I'll hold this for you while you eat," he said.

———————

"Yazooks! This is a great spear-thrower!" Tungo trotted over to Zol breathlessly.

The boys had gone to the north shore of the lake, by the ice tongue, where the air was cooler. The thick, dirty ice crackled with strange popping noises, almost as if it were alive (Ona claimed it *was* alive), and Tungo had been hurling spears into it.

113

"No wonder your father was such a good hunter," said Tungo. "With a weapon like this, I could be even *better* than him. Do you think your mother will make one for me when I ask Keena to make a hotu with me?"

Zol gasped. "Sacred Mammoth, Tungo! You haven't even gone on your first mammoth hunt yet...and Keena is just a little girl!"

"I know," said Tungo, turning red, "but someday I'm going to ask her. Ona knows already."

Zol frowned and reached for his thrower. "Give it back. It's my turn now."

"Wait. Not yet," said Tungo. "I have something to show you." He set the spear-thrower down and opened his tool bag. He pulled out a jumble of camelhair twine and small stones. "My brothers helped me make this, but it was my idea. It's a scatter tool." He held it up by a leather loop and untangled the strings, each of which had a round stone weight tied at the end. The strings were all different lengths. Tungo grinned proudly.

"What is it for?" asked Zol, retrieving his spear-thrower.

"It's for catching small animals. See that rabbit over there? Watch." Tungo took off, swinging the new weapon in circles over his head. When he let it go, it flew through the air—spreading the stones—and landed on the unsuspecting rabbit.

The scatter tool did not kill the rabbit, but stunned it and tangled its legs in strings and weights so that it could not run. Tungo ran up to the animal and ended its struggle. Then he trotted back to Zol, proudly holding the rabbit by its ears in one hand and his new tool in the other.

Zol had to admit it was a good weapon. You could use it again and again; and it did not require as much accuracy as slinging a stone because of the way it spread out when it was thrown.

"It works on geese and grouse, too," said Tungo, "even when they are flying. How do you like it?"

"Great Spirits, Tungo! How did you think of it?" Zol could not keep the admiration out of his voice.

Tungo grinned, deepening his dimples. "You know how I hate to chip points," he said, "and I always lose them. So I decided to make something that I could use over and over again." He held the scatter tool up and straightened out the strings again.

"My round sling stones gave me the idea." He showed Zol one of the weights. "I looked for some round flat ones and bored holes in them. Then I made strings out of twisted camel hair and tied them on. Works pretty good, huh?"

"Have you shown it to Yakono yet?"

"No," said Tungo. "I want to practice more with it, and then I'm going to show it to *everybody* at the Star Dance."

Zol gasped. "The Star Dance!" How could he have forgotten? Yakono had asked the boys to have something special to show the others—either a new way of doing something or a special skill they had developed—before he presented them to the clan as the newest hunters.

Tungo frowned. "You didn't forget, did you?"

Zol was bursting to tell Tungo about his encounter with the mammoth. But something held him back. He hugged the memory to himself and barely heard Tungo chattering on about his scatter tool. Being touched by the mammoth was the most exciting thing that had ever happened to him—like being touched by lightning and living to tell about it. Zol did not want Tungo to make light of it—or worse, to call him a liar!

Zol had no proof that the mammoth had touched him. But what if he went back alone and found that same mammoth with the notched ear again? Next time he would have the courage to mark her, he was sure of it. Then he would have proof.

Great Spirits! Then he would have something even *better* than Tungo's scatter tool to share at the Star Dance. He could prove once and for all that he, Zol, was indeed his father's son.

"Are your ears full of dung beetles?" shouted Tungo. He tugged at the spear-thrower and brought Zol back to the present. "I said let me practice some more with this while you try out my scatter tool, oya?"

Reluctantly, Zol let go of the spear-thrower and took the scatter tool. "Oya," he said. "But not for long; I have something important to do back at camp."

CHAPTER 26

ONA HATCHES A PLAN

Father Sun was sinking in the sky when Zol finally got his spear-thrower back from Tungo. Zol left him practicing happily with his scatter tool and ran along the lakeshore toward camp. He stopped to look across the lake at the sacred mammoth sign. The water sparkled with scattered points of light, like stars fallen from the night sky. Beyond the golden hills, jagged brown cliffs jutted into an incredibly blue sky. Great Spirits, what beauty!

But Zol's spine tingled when he remembered that between those golden hills and the rocky cliffs stood the great wall of ice—their reason for being here. Every year the mammoths came to fatten up for winter on the fresh grasses that grew in front of the melting ice wall. And every year the Star Dancers came north to find the mammoths.

Koot's screeching pulled Zol out of his thoughts. Zol saw the crow was circling over camp and wondered why Keena had set him free.

"Caw!" called Zol. "Hellooo, Koot!"

Koot flew to Zol and landed on his shoulder. He gurgled and chattered in Zol's ear.

"What happened, Koot?" asked Zol. "Why aren't you with Keena?"

When Zol trotted into camp with Koot on his shoulder, Ona glared at him and shoved the water bags at him. "We need more water," she snapped.

Keena ran up to him. "I'll go with you," she said. Her eyes were red, as though she had been crying.

"You stay right here, child! I need your help," said Ona. Her mouth was set in a grim line, and her eyes were slits. She stomped away.

"I'm sorry, Zol," whispered Keena. "It's all my fault. I fell asleep and Koot got into Ona's things again. She's furious!" She turned and ran after Ona.

While he let the water bags fill, Zol looked uplake to where he and Tungo had been practicing. The river of ice snaked into the hills as far as he could see, and from here the ice looked clean and blue in the glow of evening.

Koot pushed off from Zol's shoulder and landed on the sand by the water's edge. He ran back and forth in an agitated way.

"What is it, Koot? What do you see?"

"Koot had seen his reflection in the water and was trying to drive the intruder away. "Kuck-woo," he said, pecking fiercely at the crow in the water. It dissolved into ripples.

Zol laughed. "That's not another crow, silly, that's you!" Zol bent over the water to show Koot. He saw their reflections side by side: one shiny black crow and one slim-faced boy with high cheek bones and straight dark hair. His wide-set eyes stared back at him. "See?" he said, pointing and touching the water, "This is me...and this is you." He stroked the crow's feathers. "And I don't think either one of us is welcome back in camp right now."

"Kuck-woo!" said Koot, pecking again at the crow in the water. When it rippled away, he hopped onto Zol's shoulder and chattered contentedly.

Father Sun slipped down behind the mountains and sent a cold breeze from the ice at the head of the lake. The blue sky deepened until it was darker than the water. Star people began to twinkle one by one, and soon the star person Zol waited for—the bright one— shone over the dark ridge to the east.

"See, Koot?" said Zol pointing to the star. "That's the one. That's Father...I'm sure of it."

Koot gurgled in Zol's ear. He stretched one leg, then the other. It was past his roosting time.

Zol rubbed his cheek against the bird and stared at the star. "Is it true that crows can fly to the moon, Koot?" Zol brought Koot around to face him. "If it is, could *you* fly all the way to the star that is Father?"

Then Zol laughed at the notion. "A lot you know about being a crow." He stroked Koot's beak. Koot closed his eyes. Zol tucked his spear-thrower into his waist thong. "Come on, Koot, let's get this water back to camp."

Koot flew straight to his tree, leaving Zol behind. Zol walked slowly, carrying the full bladder bags. It had been a long, busy day and his eyelids were heavy. It would be good to sink into his furs and relive his mammoth encounter. But he stopped short when he heard Mother and Ona talking inside the hotu.

"...*enough* of that bird!" he heard Ona say. "Who ever heard of keeping a crow in a hotu? You have coddled that boy long enough. He will never become a man if he is not forced to act like one."

There was no answer from Mother.

"I have talked to my brother, and he agrees with me. For Zol's sake, we must get rid of it—now!"

"Yakono said that?" Mother sounded surprised.

"He said the time Zol spends with the bird would be better spent with Tungo, preparing himself for the hunt. Now there is a Star Dancer!" said Ona. "All *Zol* wants to do is carve toys and play with that crow. Well, his baby years are over. He must take his place in the clan now."

"I will talk to Zol tomorrow," said Mother.

"Talk, talk, talk! There has already been too much talk and not enough action. Yakono himself told Zol to get rid of that bird. And today, what do I find? That nasty crow in this hotu, tearing apart my personal belongings!"

There was no answer from Mother.

"There is no need for you to worry about it," said Ona softly. "I have already made a plan. I am sure Tungo will help us with this problem. Tungo *understands* that crows are evil."

Anger flared up inside Zol like a hot rock in his chest. He wanted to tear open the flap and lash out at Ona. And Mother! Why was she not defending him? He moved forward, then stopped. It would be better if they did not know he had heard Ona's plan. It would give him time to think. Koot was safe for the night, high in his roosting tree. But what about tomorrow?

Zol moved silently away from the hotu and hung the water bags. Then he whistled tunelessly, as if he had just arrived. It was quiet inside the hotu when he entered and lay on top of his furs. He knew that Mother and Ona just pretended to be asleep.

He lay awake for a long time, trying to decide what to do. Finally, the decision was made, and he took a deep breath and sighed. He rolled over and let the welcoming blackness of sleep wash over him.

CHAPTER 27

GO AWAY, KOOT!

The Star Dancers shook their rattles as they circled the ashes. Young Zol struggled in Yakono's arms, trying to get free. But the leader held the small boy firmly in one arm while he scooped a handful of ashes with the other. Yakono rubbed the ashes into Zol's hair and over his face; he rubbed them on the boy's neck and bare chest. Then he gently pressed both of Zol's hands, palms down, into the mound of warm ashes. The little boy sobbed.

———

Zol's eyes popped open. He lay there thinking about his dream. Then a smile spread across his face when he realized his heart was not even beating fast! It was like he had watched the dream happening to someone else. Zol stretched in his furs and picked up Father's spear-thrower by his side. It was another good omen.

Zol sat up. Quietly, he put pemmican, berry cakes and strips of dried elk meat into his tool bag. Today was the day. He pulled on his boots.

Mother stirred in her furs. "What are you doing, Zol?" she whispered.

"Tungo and I are going out with the scouts, Mother," he lied. "Don't worry if I miss the evening meal."

"Be careful," she murmured sleepily.

Zol felt guilty about lying, but he was still angry at Mother for siding with Ona against Koot. And he could *not* tell her what he was planning to do.

He slipped quietly out of the hotu into the frosty morning. The star people still twinkled in the clear, dark sky. Zol shivered, but he did not want to go back inside to get his bison robe. He would be warm once he started running, and he could move faster without it.

Zol looked up at the bright star he hoped was Father. "Father, is that you?" he whispered. "The time has come for me to prove that I am truly your son, and I need your help."

He held the spear-thrower up with both hands. It shone pale and ghostly in the moonlight. "Please send your bravery to me, your only son, through the spear-thrower you once used so courageously." He closed his eyes and gripped the handle, trying to absorb his father's spirit.

A loon called from the lake and the half-moon cast an eery glow over the camp, as Zol climbed up Koot's roosting tree. Reaching the startled bird, Zol put his hand over his beak to keep him from squawking, then backed down the tree.

In the predawn darkness, Zol and Koot sped out of camp in the direction of Stony Creek. When they got there, Zol looked for the roosting tree he had seen before. There it was. In a group of pine trees, one tree—taller than the rest—was covered with black crows.

A great noisy commotion started in the tree as Zol's approach stirred the flock from their night's roosting. Zol sat on the ground facing the tree and talked to Koot. "This had to happen sooner or later, Koot, and for your own good, it will have to be today."

"Cu-koot," said Koot, bowing on Zol's shoulder and nibbling his ear.

"I know you're interested in other crows," said Zol. "I've watched you watching them when they fly over and call to you."

Koot jumped down and pulled at the drawstring on Zol's tool bag. He knew Zol carried pemmican and root cakes in there.

"No, Koot. I'm not feeding you anymore. You have to feed yourself—all the time, now." Zol put out his hand and Koot jumped onto it. "I've got to make you understand that today you have to stay with these crows," Zol said as much to himself as to Koot. "You can't fly with me anymore."

He brought the crow up to face him and stroked the shiny black feathers. "The day you came to me was the best day of my life," he said softly. He brushed the warm body one last time against his cheek. "You probably will forget me in time, Koot, but I will never, *never* forget you."

"Awloo koot," said the crow, stepping back and forth nervously.

Zol stood up and carried him to the tall pine tree. "This is your new roosting tree, Koot," said Zol, trying to sound calm. "You have to stay here now, do you understand? Stay here!"

Koot flew up into the lower branches like he always did at camp when Zol put him to rest for the night. The crows at the top of the tree were screaming and scolding. Koot stepped back and forth, spreading out his tail feathers and rubbing the side of his head against a twig. He paid no attention to the chattering crows. His eyes were fixed on Zol, eager to play this new game.

"Stay!" said Zol, then turned and walked away without looking back. Almost immediately, he heard the rapid whirring of Koot's wings, followed by the familiar jolt as the big bird landed on his shoulder.

Patiently, Zol walked back to the tree and repeated the command to stay. Then he walked away. But as soon as he had moved away a few steps, Koot flew after him. After three more attempts, Zol knew what he had to do.

He walked back to the tree and threw Koot up between the lower branches, harshly commanding him to stay. Then he turned and ran. When he heard the whir of Koot's wings, he spun around to face him. As Koot glided down to land on his shoulder, Zol swung with his open hand and slapped the bird away—hard. Koot landed on the ground with a thump that knocked a little "caw" out of him and tore at Zol's heart. Stunned, Koot stood up facing Zol and cocked his head at him. "Koot-kom," he said.

Swallowing hard, Zol shouted, "Go away, you stupid bird!" He tried to sound like Tungo. "I don't want you anymore, can't you see that? You're just a dumb crow. I've got more important things to do...I can't be bothered with you anymore."

Heat flooded Zol's eyes, and the lump in his throat was so painful that he could not say anything else. So he just turned and stalked away. Koot did not follow. Zol peeked over his shoulder and saw the confused bird still standing in the same spot staring after him. Zol's vision blurred, and he started to run.

Hot tears spilled down Zol's cheeks as he ran. "Oh, Koot," he cried, "please forgive me...please forget me." He ran faster and faster until the pains in his throat and chest were unbearable. He had to stop and let out the gut-wrenching sobs that felt like they would tear him apart.

Dropping face down on the dry grass, Zol cried until he had no more tears. Finally, he sat up and looked back toward Stony Creek. Clouds of crows circled in the sky, but none flew toward him. He felt like there was a wide leather band inside his chest, squeezing his heart. It was hard to breathe.

CHAPTER 28

THE LONG-TOOTHED CAT

Zol chewed on a strip of dried meat and searched the morning sky. Part of him wanted desperately to see that familiar black shape flying toward him, but another part was relieved that he did not. He could not risk having Koot follow him now.

He took out his bone cup of ochre and stirred the red mixture with his finger thoughtfully. He would not want Koot to tease the young mammoth the way he did the camels! Replacing the ochre in the pouch at his waist, Zol ran toward Father Sun, who was still low in the sky.

A cat scream snapped Zol out of his thoughts. He stopped and whirled around. He could see nothing but grassy fields and big boulders. Zol was out in the open in unfamiliar territory—an easy target. He began to run faster toward the huge wall of blue ice that he now saw in the distance. There might be some protection there.

He was near the ice, when he heard the cat again—too close! Zol untied a short spear from his waist and nocked it up in Father's spear-thrower—just in case. His eyes searched the huge wall for someplace to hide. He had heard about ice caves in the great wall of ice. He was breathing hard and had a pain in his side. But he pushed himself to run faster.

The next thing Zol knew, a skinny long-toothed cat was loping along next to him! He recognized her instantly: she had one broken fang. Her mouth was open, and saliva flew from her lower jaw.

He barely had time to take all this in before he felt one of her huge paws on his back. Her claws scraped through his tunic, digging into his skin, and he went flying through the air. He landed so hard that the breath was knocked out of him, and his spear-thrower flew from his hand.

Frantically, Zol rolled over and grappled for the darts at his waist. The cat paused and stared past him. But Zol's movement caught her attention again, and she laid back her ears and snarled at him. A low, buzzing growl started in the back of her throat. Then she looked past him again. Her tail twitched. Zol followed her gaze, moving only his eyes. He saw a group of camels running near the ice wall—probably frightened by the cat's scream.

Zol tried not to breathe. He remained perfectly still, hoping the cat could not hear his heart drumming. He knew that cats, like wolves, preferred to eat grazing animals.

One baby camel lagged behind the others, nosing at something on the ground. The cat's growl got softer and she slunk forward, low to the ground. Then she sprinted in long strides toward the unlucky young camel. Zol winced when he saw her pounce on it and sink her one good fang into its neck. The camel's lanky legs buckled under; it squealed and was silent.

Zol shuddered. That could have been him!

Then he became aware of the throbbing pain in his back. The gashes must be deep because he could feel the blood dripping down his back and soaking his pants.

In spite of his pain, Zol picked up his spear-thrower and moved forward in a crouched position. The smell of his blood might attract other animals; he had to find a place to hide.

Creeping forward over rocky ground, Zol scanned the towering wall of blue and white ice for caves. It was covered with deep cracks and jagged corners, but no — yes! Zol saw a small cave! He would have to climb to get to it, but if it were deep enough he could hide until he regained enough strength to get back to camp. He looked behind him to make sure he was not leaving a trail of blood, then tucked his spear-thrower securely in his waist thong, so he would have both hands free.

Grunting with the pain and effort, Zol slowly edged his way up the side of the wall, using cracks in the ice for hand and foot holds. His legs shook so badly he had to keep stopping to rest. Finally, he got to the entrance of the dark hole and, with a last burst of energy, heaved himself partway into the cave.

He lay on the icy floor, panting. He did not feel cold, just exhausted. He hoped there were no animals living in this cave. Finally, he gathered the energy to slither farther back into the darkness of the cave and out of sight. The hole, narrow at the entrance, opened up enough for him to sit up and lean against the wall. The cold wall soothed the searing pain in his back. Holding his father's spear-thrower in both hands, Zol sighed and let his head drop forward in exhaustion.

The cat's scream brought him awake so suddenly that he banged his head on the roof of the cave. No! The cat could not have followed him. He had been careful to stay downwind and out of her sight. Wide awake now, he listened. Nothing. He must have dreamed it.

Zol took a deep breath and let it out slowly. He wondered how long he should stay in the cave. He had told Mother not to expect him for the evening meal. Nobody would be looking for him. He decided to stay hidden until Father Sun left the sky.

Zol opened his tool bag and took out some pemmican and a berry cake. He heard water dripping farther back in the cave. After eating, he would crawl back to explore and get a drink. His back now felt numb, which was a relief.

Light from the entrance hole helped Zol's eyes adjust to the darkness inside, and he began to relax. He chewed on the pemmican and looked around. For the first time he noticed scattered bones and tufts of hair. Was this cave being used by some animal after all?

When the cat screamed again, Zol knew it was not a dream. That terrifying sound bounced off the cave walls and exploded in his head like a bolt of lightning. At the same instant, something blocked the entrance and plunged Zol into complete darkness.

Zol heard muffled grunts and growls. He strained to see, but it was too dark. A sickening thought struck him: Maybe this cave belonged to the long-toothed cat, and she was dragging the baby camel back here to eat! When she saw Zol, she would surely attack him to defend her kill. What should he do?

Panic rose in Zol—and the urge to run. He gripped Father's spear-thrower and whispered, "Please, Father, send me your courage now!"

Was there another way out? He looked to the back of the cave. No light at all came from that direction.

More grunts and shuffling at the entrance. The cat must be having trouble shoving the camel's body through the small opening.

A plan flashed into Zol's mind: If he felt his way along the wall to the opening and then shoved with all his might, maybe the startled cat—along with the carcass—would tumble down the face of the ice wall. That would give Zol a chance to get out of the cave and out of her sight again.

But what if he was not strong enough to push her over the edge? Then he would just be *giving* himself to the cat. No, it was too risky.

Zol squeezed the spear-thrower. Think! Think!

But he could think of nothing else, and precious time was passing. He had to act now, while he had the advantage of surprise.

Zol tucked the spear-thrower in at his waist again and started forward on his hands and knees. He stayed close to the right wall for guidance and moved slowly, silently, toward the guttural sounds. His

heart was banging so hard against his rib cage that he could barely breathe.

Zol stopped. He took Father's spear-thrower and nocked up one of his darts. If the cat did not fall like he hoped she would, at least he would be prepared to defend himself.

With the thrower in his right hand, Zol could no longer move forward on his hands and knees. So he sat up and slowly scooted along on his seat, pushing with his left hand and pulling himself forward with his heels.

Zol kept the spear-thrower poised by his ear in the ready position. Closer and closer he crept. Now he could actually hear the cat gulping down big chunks of meat.

Zol decided that he could push with more force if he braced himself with both hands on the side walls and pushed out with his feet. But to do that, he had to be closer to the entrance, where the walls narrowed. Two more scoots forward would put him in that position.

Suddenly Zol was blinded by bright light. The cat screamed. She had lost her grip on the camel's body, and it had tumbled from the narrow ledge to the ground. She was poised to jump down after it when she saw Zol's movement.

The piercing shriek she let loose almost made Zol drop his spear-thrower. She thrust her huge head inside the entrance. Blood dripped from her open mouth. Without hesitation, Zol thrust the thrower with all his strength. The stone-tipped dart shot straight into the cat's mouth.

With a vicious snarl, the cat scrambled through the entrance and pounced on Zol. He screamed in pain as his raw back was scraped along the floor of the cave. The last thing he remembered was that the cat was not as heavy as he thought she would be. Then blackness washed over him, and he felt no more pain.

CHAPTER 29

BASKING IN GLORY

When Zol awoke, he was back in his own hotu. Mother and Yakono sat by his side. Ona stood by the doorflap, watching him and wringing her hands.

"What...?" Zol struggled to sit up, but sharp pains shot through his back and shoulder. He fell back on his furs with a groan.

Mother laid her hand on his. "You are safe now, Zol," she said. "Do not try to sit up. Here, sip some of this." She held a cup of birch tea to his lips. "Just relax and sleep. We can talk later."

Ona turned and spoke sharply to someone behind her. "No! Not yet!"

Zol heard Tungo's whiny voice. "But why? Please, Ona, I just want to see him!" He heard a scuffle as Tungo tried to push past Ona.

Zol could not yet remember why, but overpowering relief at being back at camp with his family washed over him. Gratefully, he slipped back into the nothingness of a dreamless sleep.

It was days before Zol could stay awake long enough to sit up and talk. The bitter birch tea Ona made for him dulled the pain and made him sleep. It seemed to Zol that Ona never left his side. Whenever he opened his eyes, she was there with a bowl of hot broth to feed him or a warm poultice of mashed balsam root and boiled birch bark to place on his wounds. She fussed over his furs and would not let anybody visit him except Mother and Yakono.

The day finally came when Zol was strong enough to push the broth away and sit up. "Ona," he said, "I want to know what happened to me."

Ona sat back on her heels and smiled. Her dark eyes shone with pride. "Your father would be so proud of you," she said. She shook her head. "To think that you faced that terrible long-toothed cat all by yourself!"

Then it all came back to Zol: the terror of being caught in the cave, the sounds and smells of the cat, her claws digging into his shoulder. His heart started racing, and he broke out in a sweat.

"But...but what happened to the cat? How did I get here? Did I walk back?"

Keena poked her head through the door flap. "Ona, I heard Zol talking. Can I come in?"

Ona frowned. "He is too weak, child. You know that."

But Zol waved at her. "Come here, Keena."

Keena rushed in and took Zol's hand, squeezing it hard. "Oh, Zol! I've never been so afraid in my life. When they carried you back, wrapped in that hide, I thought for sure you were dead. Then Mother and Ona started wailing."

She raised his hand to her cheek and squeezed it even harder. "It was awful! And when Koot didn't come back, I was sure it was a bad omen—that you were going to die."

"Hrmpff," said Ona quietly. "That was when I was sure he would *live*."

Koot! All the sorrow of that final parting with his friend flooded back to Zol, and he could not speak. He closed his eyes. Too much. It was all too much to think about.

"See?" said Ona sharply. "I told you he was not strong enough. Now you have tired him out. Go! Go, little one." Ona shooed Keena out of the hotu with her hands.

Zol was vaguely aware of Ona fussing over him and muttering to herself. But he was far away, at Stony Creek with Koot. That memory brought more pain to Zol's heart than the cat's claws had to his back. A lump rose to his throat when he remembered Koot's confused expression as his "mother" turned against him.

Where was Koot now, Zol wondered. Had he been accepted by the other crows? A tear slipped out the corner of Zol's eye, and he turned his head to hide it from Ona. She could never understand his feelings for that bird.

He drifted off to sleep again. But this time he dreamed that old familiar dream of crows circling overhead against a clear blue sky.

Loud arguing outside the hotu woke Zol. Tungo insisted on talking to Zol, and Ona would not let him.

"But my brother was one of the scouts who carried him back," argued Tungo. "He told me that Zol killed a big cat by himself. I don't believe it. I just want to hear it from Zol's own mouth. Then I'll leave." Zol heard a scuffle, as if Tungo had tried to push past Ona.

"No! I tell you he is not strong enough to talk about it yet. There will be plenty of time to talk when he is well."

"But what was he doing there at the ice wall all by himself? And where is his stupid crow? Didn't anybody ask him that?"

Suddenly, a warm feeling began to spread through Zol's insides, like ice melting. The realization of what he had done ran to all parts of his body, even out to his fingertips and toes. His dart had found its mark...the cat was dead. Zol grinned. He, Zol, had killed a long-toothed cat!

He could not wait to see Tungo's face when he told him the whole story. But not now. Still smiling, Zol sank back into a peaceful sleep.

CHAPTER 30
THE CAT'S FANG

Zol sat outside the hotu on his flat rock for the first time since his return to camp. His wounds were healing, and he felt stronger. Mother sat across from him, chipping stone while Zol polished the cat's long tooth. He was preparing to bore a hole through the top of it with his stone drill. He had already made a sinew string so he could wear it around his neck. He could hardly believe it: first the fox tail and now this!

As he rubbed the tooth gently with his polishing rock, Zol studied it closely. It was a tool of death, that was for sure. Longer than Zol's hand, the tooth was not round, but flattened and tapered to a point like a knife. But instead of being straight, like a knife, it was curved.

This very tooth, thought Zol, may have once sunk deep into the hide of a mammoth. He shuddered. And it very nearly sank into mine!

Once again the reality of what he had done sent a warm flash through Zol. Pride sparkled inside him like sunlight on a crystal rock.

"You are smiling again, Zol," said Mother. She stopped working and smiled back at him.

"I was just thinking, Mother. The long-toothed cat can kill a mammoth by sinking its fangs into the mammoth's neck."

He held up the tooth. "Look. If this tooth were straightened out, it would look like one of our knives, only longer. What if we made a *spear point* as long as this cat's tooth, but straight? Wouldn't it go deeper into the mammoth and do more harm?"

"Hmmm. Maybe on the long thrusting spears," said Mother, "but it would be very heavy for the short spears that are thrown."

"I guess you're right," said Zol. But he decided to make one anyway while he was recuperating. If a spear point this long *could* be thrown, then no Star Dancer would have to run underneath the mammoth to kill it. He would try it out himself when he was strong enough to run again.

Zol continued polishing the tooth. It was nice to be here alone with Mother. Ona and Keena were off collecting berries. And ever since he was well enough to have visitors, there had been a steady stream of Star Dancers coming to see him and wish him well.

Zol finally learned how the scouts had found him in the cave: They were searching for the mammoth herd near the ice wall when they heard the long-toothed cat's scream. Thinking it might have just killed a mammoth, the scouts ran to investigate. They saw the camel carcass on the ground and followed the trail of blood into the cave.

"Imagine the scouts' surprise," Ona had said, her eyes sparkling, "to find that savage cat lying dead next to my grandson."

Tapping him on the chest gently with a gnarled finger, she had exclaimed, "To think that your sharp spear point went right through the roof of that cat's mouth and into its brain!" She rocked back on her heels. "And now you are the youngest Star Dancer *ever* to kill a long-toothed cat. I always knew you would be a great hunter," she said, pursing her lips and nodding.

Zol shook his head now and smiled again, remembering that conversation. These days Ona poured praises on him like she used to on Tungo. Maybe that was the *real* reason Tungo had not come to visit him again. Keena said it was because he had been sick with a bad cold.

Keena and Ona came back into camp now, carrying baskets of berries. Keena's face lit up when she saw Zol outside, and she brought her basket over to offer him some of the dark blue berries. She sat down next to him while he ate his fill.

When Mother went to help Ona, Keena asked softly, "Zol, where's Koot? Mother and Ona told me not to talk about it, but I have to know. Did the cat kill him?" Her big eyes were full of sadness.

Zol could not look at her when he answered. "I showed him a tree full of crows near Stony Creek," he said. "And that ungrateful Koot liked the crows better than me! He wouldn't come when I called. And then, of course, I ran into the long-toothed cat."

He finally looked at Keena and tried to sound light-hearted. "I guess Ona was right; crows have no sense of loyalty."

Keena did not say anything. She just put her small hand over Zol's and squeezed it. Then she got up and took her basket over to Mother and Ona.

Zol suddenly felt tired, and a painful ache filled his insides. He set the tooth aside and went into the hotu for a nap.

Tungo came to visit that very afternoon, when Zol was awake and outside again, boring a hole in his cat tooth.

"Ho, Zol," said Tungo.

"Ho, Tungo. I was wondering when you were going to come and see me again."

Tungo coughed. "I've had a really bad cold," he said. He put out his hand. "Let's see the tooth."

Zol handed it to him.

Tungo held it up to the light and turned it around in his hands. "Sort of yellow, isn't it? I guess that's because the cat was so old." He fingered the tooth that hung around his neck. "See how shiny and white mine is?"

Zol took back his tooth and continued working on it.

"You know," said Tungo, "my brothers are still laughing about that scrawny old cat. They said it probably died from fright when it found you hiding in its cave." He laughed.

Zol felt his face get hot. He pulled the tunic off his shoulders. "She was strong enough to do this!" said Zol.

Tungo's eyes widened when he saw the angry red scars on Zol's shoulder. But then his eyes narrowed again and Tungo snorted. "They didn't even bother to bring that old cat back to camp," he said. "My brothers said it was just a sack of bones covered with matted hair— not even enough meat to feed the dogs. The only reason they brought the head back was because they knew you'd want that old yellow fang."

"Well, they were right," said Zol. He clamped the tooth hard between his knees and continued boring a hole in it by rubbing the stone drill between his hands. Then he said, "I saved the eyes for you, but I guess you wouldn't want the eyes of a scrawny old cat hanging around your neck."

Tungo looked surprised. He licked his lips, then ran his hand across his nose and mouth. "Where are they?" he asked.

"Why?" asked Zol. He knew Tungo wanted those eyes. "I'll just throw them away."

"No!" said Tungo. "I mean, if they aren't *too* milky, maybe I could add them to my collection. I'm going to show it at the Star Dance."

"Well, you wouldn't want these. They're all yellow," said Zol smiling. "I guess that's because she was so old."

"Stop it, Zol!" Tungo's face got red. "I didn't know you were going to give me the eyes when I said that. I *do* want them!"

Zol laughed out loud. It was the first time he had laughed since the morning he had left with Koot. "Come on," he said, standing up. "I've got them drying behind the hotu."

Zol was feeling generous. Besides, Tungo had just given him an idea of what he could do at the Star Dance.

CHAPTER 31

ZOL'S SECRET

Zol pulled the rocks out of the fire pit with two sticks. One rock had exploded in the intense heat, but the others had turned a deeper color. The red chert now had a nice, waxy sheen to it. After it cooled, he knocked a flake off with his hammer and felt the sharp edges. Mother was right: treating the rocks with heat made them harder and sharper. Zol held the piece up and saw how light came through it. It made them prettier, too, he thought.

Two days earlier, Zol had dug the pit for the rocks. Then, following Mother's directions, he had covered them with a thick layer of sandy soil from the lake and built a wood fire over it. Even though the days were hot, Zol kept the fire going day and night, adding fuel when the fire burned down to coals.

It was already hot this morning. Zol slipped out of his tunic, but left on his hide pants to protect his legs. He chose a nice piece of red chert and sat down on his flat rock to work.

Tungo had his amazing, new scatter tool to show at the Star Dance. But it was for small animals. Zol was going to make a special tool for killing mammoths.

The stone points the hunters used for mammoths now were about as long as Zol's hand. Yet they barely penetrated the thick hair and tough hide of the mammoth. In order to bring it to its knees, Star Dancers had to run underneath that huge animal and thrust upward with the spear, slashing into the softer underbelly...and that is how Father had died.

Zol was going to make a spear point as long and sharp as the long-toothed cat's fang—a tool of death that would slice through the outer layers of the mammoth's hide and pierce the internal organs. If it worked, and could be launched with a spear-thrower, no Star Dancer would have to risk being crushed to death under the beast.

As he worked, Zol thought about his encounter with the young mammoth. More than ever, he was sure it was an omen. He, Zol, had been touched by both the mammoth *and* the long-toothed cat—and lived! He was convinced there was a reason for it. He had been given a sign.

As the morning wore on, stone chips piled up around Zol's feet. If Koot were here, thought Zol, he would be squawking in delight and strutting around with colorful chips in his beak to hide with his other treasures.

A painful ache welled up inside of Zol. Oh how he wished he could hear the crow gurgling and cooing in his ear right now. He would run his hand over that sleek, feathered body and tell him all about his new idea.

"Why is my grandson wearing such a long face?" asked Ona. She was sitting in front of the hotu, cutting the dried heads off of sunflowers and rubbing out the seeds. She set aside her basket of sunflowers and wiped the perspiration from her brow. Little wisps of grey hair stuck to her face like spider webs.

"It is too hot for this work," she said. "How would my young hunter like to help me gather lake potatoes?" She grinned her toothless grin at Zol. "I think the tubers are ready."

Zol chuckled. The only thing funnier than watching Ona dance at the Star Dance was watching her gather lake potatoes—the tubers of the arrowhead plant that grew around the edges of the lake.

At summer's end, when the days were hot like today, Star Dancers waded in the cool water and dug the round tubers out of the mud with their feet. Later, they either roasted and ate them fresh or boiled and dried them to keep for the winter.

Zol grinned back at Ona. "The scabs on my wounds are itching like fly bites," he said. "The cold water would feel good on my back. I think Tungo and Keena went to the lake earlier."

Ona stumbled awkwardly to her feet, almost falling forward. Zol jumped up to help her. Her stiffness was getting worse every day, even in this warm weather. She never complained, but Zol often saw her grimace in pain when she thought nobody was looking.

"Well, come on then, hurry!" she said. "We do not want them to get all the good ones."

Zol kept a hand under Ona's sharp elbow as she hobbled beside him to the lake. Walking next to her, Zol noticed for the first time that he was looking *down* at his grandmother's bent head. Mother had exclaimed that he was shooting up like a sapling this summer; it must be true. Zol straightened his shoulders and stood even taller.

They did not have to worry about Tungo and Keena getting all the tubers. Those two were laughing and splashing about in the water, but not one lake potato lay on the pebbly beach beside them.

Once in the water, Ona squealed like a young girl. The water's buoyancy allowed her to move more freely, and she danced around in the soft mud, expertly digging up the egg-size tubers with her toes and throwing them onto the beach behind them.

"See how this old grandmother can dig circles around you young ones? I will bet that I can dig more lake potatoes than the three of you together." Her face broke into gleeful wrinkles. "In fact, as Father Sun is my witness, if I cannot, then I myself will hand over my amber piece to the one of you that has the biggest pile."

With that challenge, Tungo and Zol hooted and started shoving each other and splashing to get to the best spots. Keena joined in, but

the children were no match for Ona. In the midst of all the laughing, splashing and screaming, she continued to calmly throw the tubers over her shoulder, one by one, until her pile on the beach was three times the size of theirs.

When they finally collapsed on the beach, exhausted, Ona cackled gleefully, "I see my amber piece is still safe."

"How did you do that?" exclaimed a breathless Keena.

"It's just because she has longer toes than the rest of us," said Tungo seriously. That sent them all off into peals of laughter again.

Unable to speak, Keena squeaked, "Look!" and pointed to Tungo's pitiful pile of potatoes. All his tubers were small, and most of them were smashed because he had stepped on them with his clumsy feet. That made them laugh even harder.

"If your toes were as long as your fingers, you still could not keep up with me," boasted Ona, wiping her eyes. "I talk to the tubers...they know me and come to me." She pointed to her pile again and nodded. "See?"

But the next morning Ona was so stiff and sore that she could not even get up for the morning greeting. Mother had to rub oil of sage into her muscles while the old woman lay on her furs. Keena fixed the morning meal of sunflower-seed mush, berries, and trout.

Yakono came by to visit his sister. "Did you forget, Ona, that you are an old woman, now, and not a young girl?"

Even though she could barely move without groaning, Ona forced herself up on one elbow and glared at Yakono. "I will never be as old as you, old man," she croaked. Then she collapsed back on her furs.

Zol stared at Ona in disbelief. Nobody dared to talk to Yakono like that! But the leader just chuckled at her, then turned a serious face to Zol.

"Are you prepared for the Star Dance, Zol?"

Zol swallowed hard and looked into Yakono's stern face. "I am working on something new to show to the hunters," he said.

"Ahhh." said Yakono. "I am sure the son of Yul will come up with something fine. And do not forget about the opening ceremony. I am counting on you and Tungo to prepare the torches."

Yakono placed a big hand on Zol's shoulder. "Have your cat wounds healed?" he asked gently.

In answer, Zol pulled up his tunic to show him.

"Good," said Yakono, "because the scouts have found the mammoth herd and are keeping them in sight. "We will have the Star Dance in two days. After that, we will go after our mammoth."

Yakono smiled at Zol. "I want to make sure that our youngest hunter will be with us." He patted Zol lightly on the shoulder and left.

Two days? Zol could finish the spear point by then, and maybe haft it. But that left no time to try it out. He had not even practiced with his spear-thrower lately, because his back and shoulder were so sore.

Two days! Could he be ready by then?

CHAPTER 32

THE STONE TOOTH

The stone tooth, as Zol began to think of it, was harder to make than he expected. To start with, knocking a large enough flake off the core rock with his hammer was very hard to do. And if he got a flake that was long enough, it was usually too thick to shape into the slicing tool that he wanted. Thinning it out was tricky too, he discovered, and he had ruined many pieces before finally getting a decent piece to work with.

Repeatedly, as he worked, Zol picked up the fang that he now wore around his neck and examined it for size and shape.

Mother watched closely, with interest. She could not really help him because she had never attempted to make a tool like this. But she encouraged him.

Zol wanted to keep the tool a secret—especially from Tungo—until the Star Dance. That was hard because Tungo kept finding excuses to hang around the hotu. Zol was getting nervous; time was running out. He wanted to impress the other hunters, but more than that he wanted to prove himself to Yakono.

The Star Dance was tomorrow night! Zol still had to chip long grooves on both sides of the stone tooth. The grooves, shooting up from the base, would cradle the willow spear shaft he had already prepared. Then he would haft the stone tooth to the shaft by winding sinew tightly around the base.

After that he wanted to practice with his spear-thrower to make sure it was not too heavy to hurl accurately. Perspiration ran down Zol's temples. He knew if his hand slipped, and he ruined this point, there would be no time to start over again.

Irritable gruntings broke into Zol's thoughts. He looked up to see Tungo struggling into camp under a large bundle of dried mullein stalks.

"You were supposed to help me with these, Zol," complained Tungo. He dumped the pile of stalks at Zol's feet.

"Ho, Tungo," said Zol, slipping the stone tooth into his tool bag before Tungo could see it. "Sorry. I forgot."

"You forgot?" Perspiration ran down Tungo's flushed face. "The Star Dance is tomorrow night! How could you forget?"

"I was busy making something," said Zol.

Tungo pulled his tunic off and wiped his face with it. "What are you making? Keena said you were cooking rocks over here." He snorted. "Is that the big secret you're planning for the Star Dance? My brothers are going to love hearing about how to cook rocks!" He slapped his legs and laughed.

"Come on," said Zol, reaching for one of the tall, brown seed stalks. "We'd better get started." He started stripping the broad, fuzzy leaves off the stalks.

"Why won't you show me what you're making for the Star Dance," whined Tungo. "I showed you my scatter tool before anybody else saw it."

"But you didn't show it to me until it was finished and you had tried it out," answered Zol. "My idea might not work. There's nothing to show until it's finished."

That seemed to satisfy Tungo's curiosity. He picked up a stalk and started stripping leaves too. They worked in silence until they had a big pile of seed stalks, with bare stems.

The boys melted mammoth fat in a deep, bone bowl over Zol's bed of coals. Then they dipped the head of each stalk until the seeds were soaked with fat and hung them on a rack in the shade to drip until the fat hardened.

"It sure is nice not to worry about that dumb crow diving at me," said Tungo. He was sitting cross-legged on the ground, tearing green willow into thin strips for lashing the stalks together.

"I miss him," said Zol. "I just hope he's alright, wherever he is."

The boys continued working in silence.

Finally Tungo stood up and brushed himself off. "Well, that's all we can do until the fat hardens, so I'm going back to my own hotu. I'm making another scatter tool, and I want to finish it before the Star Dance." He sneered. "Good luck with your cooked rocks."

Zol watched Tungo leave, then quickly pulled out his stone tooth and went back to work on it.

Father Sun was low in the sky when a flock of noisy crows landed on Koot's pine tree by the hotu. Zol's heart fluttered when he saw them, and he looked anxiously for signs of Koot. But none of the shiny black birds flew toward him. He had to force himself not to call out.

Ona hobbled out of the hotu. "Shoo! Shoo! Get away!" She waved her walking stick feebly at the tree full of crows. She was still sore, but forced herself to move around. She was determined not to miss the Star Dance.

She hobbled slowly over to Zol and sat next to him. "If you are not careful, those nasty crows will ruin your torches," she warned.

"I'll watch them," said Zol, not looking up from his work.

They sat together quietly. Ona watched Zol shoot long flakes of stone expertly from the base up the center of the stone tooth, making the long grooves that would hold it in place on the willow shaft.

"Do not pay attention to Tungo," she said finally. "I heard what he said to you." She poked Zol on the arm. "Nobody is laughing at my grandson." She pursed her wrinkled lips. "That boy is just afraid you will show him up at the Star Dance."

"I don't think so, Ona." said Zol. "His scatter tool is truly amazing. I'm not even sure *my* idea will work."

Ona nodded her head. "It will work," she said firmly. She struggled to stand up. "Now that the evil crow has left you, your luck will change." She patted him on the shoulder. "You will see."

Leaning on her walking stick, Ona slowly made her way back to the hotu. "And do not forget," she called over her shoulder, "you are your father's son."

It was too dark, now, for Zol to see what he was doing, so he put his tools down and sat there listening to the crickets. One by one, the star people appeared in the darkening sky. He waited until his bright star appeared in the eastern sky.

"If my idea works, Father," he said to the star, "then no Star Dancer will ever again have to die like you did."

The star twinkled back at him.

CHAPTER 33

STAR DANCE

Zol sat with Tungo in front of the cooking fire at Tungo's hotu. They were alone and jittery. Everyone else was already at the Star Dance. The boys had been told to wait until they were summoned.

Tungo nervously made last-minute adjustments to his scatter tool, while Zol rehearsed in his mind what he would say about his stone tooth. Their pile of torches lay on the ground, nearby, ready to light.

Finally, a young boy ran up to them, wide-eyed and breathless. "It is time for you to come," he said importantly. Then he spun around and ran back into the darkness.

Tungo jumped to his feet and picked up the torches. He handed two to Zol. Holding one in each hand, the boys inhaled deeply and looked at each other before touching the torches to the fire. Once they were lit, Zol and Tungo knew there was no turning back; they were on their way to becoming mammoth hunters.

The torches flared up instantly when touched to the fire. The flames would now burn slowly and steadily down the stalks until they reached the green willow lashings, where they would sputter out.

Zol and Tungo trotted quickly to the gathering place and found the people sitting silently in a large half-circle around the dark pile of wood that would become their campfire.

As planned, the boys continued in a circle around the outside of the gathering, stopping to place their torches one by one in the piles of rocks prepared for that purpose earlier in the day.

After the last torch was placed, the people began to shake bone rattles filled with animal teeth, bird beaks, and seeds. Zol and Tungo continued running in the circle, letting themselves fall into the rhythm created by the rattles.

Then the people began to hum—low at first, then louder; the rattling got faster. This was not like the humming at morning greeting, where everyone hummed his own special tune. Tonight the people all hummed the same tune, passed down to them from ancient Star Dances.

The humming grew to almost a roar, and the rattling became urgent as the torches burned down. Then—just before they sputtered out—Zol and Tungo grabbed them up again and touched them to the campfire. With a giant whoosh, the pile came to life and the people cheered.

Camels, attracted by the music and rhythms, moved in from the shadows and watched at the edge of the firelight.

The boys stood together, breathing hard and feeling the intense heat of the fire at their backs. Then Yakono stood and placed a hand on the shoulder of each boy.

"It is my great honor to welcome these two into our brotherhood of hunters tonight," said Yakono in a booming voice. "We expect great things from each of them when they become hunters for the Star Dancers."

He turned to Tungo. "Tungo's brothers among our finest hunters.

And this young man—at only eleven summers—has already proven himself to be at *least* as competent as his brothers. If they are not careful, he may outshine them before long."

A ripple of laughter went through the clan and Tungo almost glowed in the firelight. Zol thought he could actually see him grow taller under Yakono's hand.

Then Zol felt Yakono's grip on his own shoulder. "And Zol, here, is the only son of Yul," he continued, "who we all know was the most courageous hunter in the memory of Star Dancers until his tragic death. At that time Zol became a son to all of us, and we have all watched him develop extraordinary powers with animals and stone."

Yakono turned Zol around and pulled up his tunic. A murmur rose at the sight of the ugly cat scars. "Even before becoming a hunter," said the leader, "Zol faced the long-toothed cat alone—and lived to tell about it. He now carries the marks of the cat on his back," he continued, "as proof that he has already stepped into his father's footprints."

The murmur turned into a cheer, and Zol felt he would burst with pride at the words of his leader. He could see Mother's face beaming at him in the fire's glow.

"And now," continued Yakono, "each of the boys has something that he has developed on his own to show us."

They had agreed beforehand that Tungo would go first because he was so eager. So Tungo immediately held up his scatter tool and began talking rapidly about the advantages of using it instead of a sling for smaller animals.

"Now I will show you how it works," said Tungo proudly. He motioned to his older brother, who released a live rabbit he had been holding between his legs in a hide bag. The frightened animal scampered in front of the fire, wildly searching for cover. But Tungo expertly threw his scatter tool and ensnared the rabbit.

The younger boys leaned forward, eyes wide and mouths open. The older hunters looked at each other, smiling and nodding. When Tungo held the rabbit up triumphantly, there was wild cheering and clapping. His brothers pounded him on the back and pulled him down to sit among them with the hunters in the first row.

Then there was a hush, and Zol stood alone. He felt naked, standing there in front of the whole clan. He quickly unwrapped his stone tooth and said, "I call this new spear point a stone tooth. It is the same size and shape as the long-toothed cat's fang—only straight instead of curved."

He held up the fang he wore around his neck. "If a long-toothed cat can kill a mammoth by stabbing into its neck with these fangs, then I think it is possible for Star Dancers—using spear points as long as the cat's tooth—to kill the mammoth in the same way."

Dead silence came from the people gathered in front of Zol. The hunters in the front row looked at each other with a puzzled expression. Tungo leaned forward, with his hand over his mouth to stifle a laugh, and jabbed one of his brothers with his elbow. Zol felt a hot flush creeping up his face, but he continued.

"I have not been able to try it out yet," he admitted, "but if this stone tooth can be hurled accurately with a spear-thrower, then hunters could throw it at the mammoth's head and neck from a distance. That way nobody would have to run underneath the mammoth to make the first jab with the long spear."

Silence. Something must be wrong, thought Zol. What is it? Finally one of Tungo's brothers spoke up.

"Anybody can stand back and throw a spear," he said. "But running under the mammoth tests the *courage* of a Star Dancer. That is why we compete to be the one chosen to do it."

He draped his arm around Tungo's shoulder. "If Zol is afraid to run under the mammoth, then maybe he doesn't really *want* to follow in his father's footprints." He looked around at the other hunters and grinned. "Maybe Zol wants to stay in camp and chip stones with his mother!"

There was a ripple of laughter, and Zol wished the ground would open up and swallow him. How could he have been so blind? Why had he not seen that dashing under the mammoth was a test of courage? That had never occurred to him!

Yakono stood up and said, "That is a most unusual and interesting idea, Zol, and I thank you for showing it to us." He frowned at Tungo's brother. "We will discuss the idea further and test it ourselves with the spear-throwers." Then he signaled the musicians, who began to play their bone flutes, accompanied by lively rattling.

Ona was the first person up. She was still stiff, but she grabbed Yakono's hand and shouted, "This is the man who told me I was too old to dig lake potatoes. Now I will show *him* who is too old to dance!" Everyone laughed, and the Star Dance began.

Gratefully, Zol sank down on the ground with his stone tooth and stared straight ahead. Women began to set out the special foods they had prepared for the occasion. Normally this was Zol's favorite part of a Star Dance; tonight it did not interest him.

The camels at the edge of the light apparently decided to stay. With squeals and grunts, they folded under their long legs and lowered themselves to the ground.

Zol moved away from the firelight into darkness. He sat quietly, wishing he could disappear. But Mother found him and sat on the ground next to him. "Zol," she said cheerfully, "you are more like your father every day—always thinking of new ways to do things."

He knew she was trying to make him feel better. "I *know* it is a good idea, Mother," said Zol. "Why can't they see it? Yakono, himself, says the wolf taught us how to pull down the mammoth. Why can't we learn from the cat, too? Father would be alive today if he had not run under the mammoth's belly."

Mother squeezed his hand. "Just give the hunters time to get used to such a new idea." She poked him playfully. "Maybe you are the one to show them how." She stood up and pulled Zol up with her. "Now come. This is a Star Dance, and you must dance."

Zol resisted at first, but the happy atmosphere was contagious, and soon he was dancing and laughing with the rest. He even laughed at himself when Tungo's brothers teased him some more about his stone tooth.

By the time the campfire went out, the full moon was overhead, lighting the surrounding yellow hills like mid-day.

Yakono raised his hand and shouted, "Zol! Tungo! It is time for the torches."

Immediately, the boys ran to Tungo's hotu, gathered up the rest of the torches, and ran back. They passed them out to the hunters, keeping one each for themselves.

The hunters formed a circle around the glowing coals of the campfire and waited. From this spot, on a rise above the lake, they could see the sacred mammoth sign clearly in the moonlight. Yakono said, "The scouts have been watching the herd. It is time. Two days from this night we will go after the mammoth."

The hunters cheered. Zol's heart beat faster.

Yakono pointed to the sacred mammoth sign. "But first, we must visit Mother Mammoth and thank her for letting us take one of her own so that we may live. We will set our torches in her body tonight, just as we sink our spears into her flesh at the hunt. Only by doing this, will her spirit be with us." Then the leader touched his torch to the coals and everyone else did the same.

With Yakono leading, the hunters held their torches high and trotted quickly down the hill toward the mammoth sign. Once there, Zol was surprised to find that up close it looked nothing at all like a mammoth.

But the hunters solemnly circled the sacred shape and placed the torches in rock piles that were still there from previous seasons. Then they waited.

Yakono raised both hands and chanted in a sing-song voice, "Mother Mammoth, the Star Dancers call to you with thankful hearts. You keep us balanced on this earth. You give us your flesh and bone. You keep us alive. It is time, now, for us to take one of your own to become one with us—to become our flesh and bone. Thank you, Mother Mammoth. Thank you for giving us life."

Zol and Tungo stood quietly with the hunters and watched the torches burn down. Then, just as quietly, they followed the hunters back to the Star Dance. There, children who could not stay awake lay asleep on the ground or in their mothers' arms. Others danced and sang while the moon followed Father Sun's path across the clear night sky.

When the moon hung low in the western sky, and one spot glowed over the eastern ridge, the exhausted Star Dancers waited to greet Father Sun together, then went back to their hotus to sleep.

In spite of his humiliation in front of everyone at the Star Dance, Zol felt good when he dropped onto his furs. The hunters had rejected his stone tooth, yes, but they had accepted *him*. Zol was now a mammoth hunter.

CHAPTER 34

PREPARING FOR THE HUNT

The next night, Zol and Tungo were summoned to a meeting of the hunters. Feeling self-conscious, the boys found a place and sat close together in the circle of men sitting around Yakono's campfire. There was none of the usual joking and story-telling. Even Tungo's jovial and boisterous brothers were serious.

Tungo's oldest brother, Nuba, had spotted a mammoth with an injured foot. He had been watching it daily, he reported, for almost a full moon. He had noticed that the lame animal was lagging farther behind the herd every day. He believed it should be their target.

The hunters agreed, and Yakono chose Nuba to run under the mammoth to give the first fatal jab with a long spear. That would be the signal for the others to close in from all sides with their own spears.

Tungo jabbed Zol in the ribs with his elbow. He had been bragging to Zol that his brother was sure to be chosen for that honor.

Then Yakono turned his stern face to the youngest hunters. His eyes shone hard and black as obsidian in the firelight. "This is your first mammoth hunt," he said to Tungo and Zol. "You must watch and listen and learn, but you must *not* act on your own." He looked directly at Tungo. "At this first hunt, you will not take part in the actual kill. Is that understood?"

The boys nodded solemnly, and Zol let out a breath he did not know he had been holding.

"You will carry your spear-throwers and spears, but you will *not* use them," Yakono emphasized again. "You must be as quiet as hares, as still as fawns in springtime." He turned his gaze to Zol.

No hint of a smile crossed the leader's lips or softened his look. "Our meat chamber is empty and waiting to be filled," he said. "If we do not get a mammoth at this sacred place, we could starve during the long winter months. The survival of the Star Dancers depends on a successful mammoth hunt."

Yakono's mouth was a straight line. "If any young, inexperienced hunter alerts the herd to our presence too soon or in *any* way becomes an obstacle to a clean, swift kill, he will be severely punished by the whole clan." His eyes gripped Zol's. "I, myself, will give the order, and I promise you that person will wish he had not been born."

Zol's heart thudded. Tungo shifted uncomfortably next to him. All the hunters were staring at them, and their stern expressions made it clear: They agreed with Yakono and were prepared to carry out whatever punishment he ordered.

Yakono stood and raised his arms. The firelight cast a shadow on his face. "We leave tomorrow before the morning greeting—and may Mother Mammoth be with us!"

A cheer rose from the hunters as they scrambled to their feet. Zol and Tungo looked at each other. For once, Tungo was quiet. Zol actually thought he saw fear in the boy's eyes. "I'll see you tomorrow," said Tungo in a small voice. Then he stood up and joined his brothers.

Returning to his own hotu, Zol's eyes automatically scanned the silhouette of Koot's roosting tree. His heart fluttered when he saw movement near the top, then sank when he realized it was only the wind.

More than ever, Zol wanted to feel Koot's strong claws grip his shoulders. He wanted to run his hand over the crow's shiny warm feathers and hear those gurgling coos of encouragement in his ear.

It suddenly occurred to Zol that he had forced Koot to do the same thing that Zol was now being forced to do: face the real world before he was ready. He could no longer hide in the safety of this hotu of women. Like Koot, Zol now had to join his own kind.

But had Koot survived? Zol gazed at his bright star. He picked up Father's spear-thrower and held it up toward the star. "I do not have Koot with me, Father, but I carry your spear-thrower," he whispered. "Please run with me tomorrow."

The star twinkled.

CHAPTER 35

MAMMOTH HUNT

Zol tossed and turned on his furs. He was awake when Tungo pulled aside the flap of his hotu long before light. "I can't sleep," Tungo whispered. "Come outside."

When Zol stepped out, he saw that the clear skies of last night had disappeared. A thick fog hung over the camp, and he could not even see the other shelters. He shivered.

The boys built up the fire and started water boiling. Tungo was quiet, and Zol wondered if he was scared, too. They sliced hunks of elk meat from last night's meal and sat by the fire chewing on the cold meat while they waited for morning. Zol's stomach felt like a snake was coiling inside.

Suddenly Tungo blurted, "Did you see Yakono's face last night? What terrible punishment was he talking about? Do you think my brothers would *kill* me if he ordered them to?" Tungo's face was grey as ash.

Zol's stomach tightened even more. He could not swallow the meat he was chewing, so he spit it out. "I don't know," he said. "But Great Spirits, Tungo, don't do anything stupid to find out!"

"Speaking of stupid, Zol! Why didn't you tell me what you were working on for the Star Dance? I could have told you it was a stupid idea." Tungo was himself again. "Now everyone is laughing at you."

Zol's face got hot. "It is *not* a stupid idea!" He opened his tool bag and took out his stone tooth. "Look. I hafted it yesterday and practiced throwing it with my spear-thrower. It works—I made two heart hits!"

"Let me see it," said Tungo.

Zol hesitated and then handed it to him.

Tungo bounced it in his hand. "It's heavy," he said.

"I know," admitted Zol. "It takes practice." He did not want to tell Tungo how many times he had thrown it before learning to make allowance for the extra weight. His arm and shoulder still ached.

Then a strange jerk in his chest alerted him to footsteps coming their way in the fog. The boys looked at each other. Zol grabbed his stone tooth back from Tungo and jumped up. It was time to go; they were ready.

Once he started running with the hunters, Zol's tension slipped away and excitement grew in its place. They ran with a steady pace— like the dogs who ran with them. The thrill of the hunt was contagious. The spear-thrower felt comfortable in his hand—like it fit him. Zol was taking his rightful place among the Star Dancers, just as his father had before him. His muscles felt warm and fluid. Everything would be fine...all he had to do was watch.

At sunrise, the hunters paused to rest and give the morning greeting. Through the dense fog, Father Sun was visible only as a veiled ball of light on the horizon.

But as the morning wore on, Father Sun burned away the fog and revealed a breath-taking autumn day. Hills of golden grass rippled into the distance as far as Zol could see. Clumps of dwarf birches flamed red in the gullies, and bright yellow aspens and willows sparkled along the stream. To the west, white mountain peaks jutted into the brilliant blue sky. The air was crisp. On a day like this, Zol felt like he could run all day and not get tired. He was happy to be alive. Great Spirits! Why had he been afraid?

All too soon, Yakono put his hand up, and the hunters stopped. Their leader did not say a word, just pointed north. The great wall of blue ice was visible in the distance, and in front of it were brown spots moving slowly. Yakono motioned to the two oldest hunters, who would stay back with the dogs and sledges; the rest moved forward.

Brown woolly mammoths browsed along a melting stream that ran from the ice wall. Zol had not told anyone about his earlier encounter with the young mammoth. Vividly, he remembered the rigid fear that had gripped him then—and the tingle of the mammoth's touch.

He quickly scanned the herd to see if he could find her—the small mammoth with the torn ear. He hoped she was not the lame animal that Nuba had been watching.

Yakono motioned them all down, to sit and watch. Zol knew the hunters would study the herd until all the signs were right.

One mammoth seemed more wary than the rest. While the others grazed, she flicked her small ears and lifted her head often, raising her trunk and scenting into the breeze. Her long white tusks almost crossed in front of her face.

She was probably the mother of the herd, thought Zol. He knew that if she sensed danger, or if one of the herd were hurt, she would trumpet a warning to the others. Then they would bunch together for protection and prepare to charge the enemy.

That was why they had to be so quiet and stay downwind. The hunters did not want to alert the herd before they were ready to attack.

"All we have to do is wait," Yakono had told them at the meeting last night. "Mammoths have no fear of humans. To those giants we probably look like weak, puny creatures who are incapable of harming them."

Zol could feel the tension growing when Nuba pointed out the target mammoth. Slightly smaller than the rest, she limped badly as she browsed on the stream-fed grasses—unaware of the hunters who silently watched. But she was too close to the herd. Zol knew they would have to wait until the herd moved on, leaving the injured animal behind.

As the morning wore on, the distance between the mammoth and the herd widened. Zol and Tungo stayed together and took their cues from the hunters. Finally, when the herd was far enough away, Yakono raised his arm and gave the signal to attack.

The hunters crouched low and moved in steadily and silently on the animal. Without speaking, Zol and Tungo did the same. The men signaled to each other with hand movements and worked together like a pack of wolves surrounding the prey.

Suddenly the lame mammoth stopped chewing. She raised her trunk and scented the air as if she knew something was wrong. She turned away from the stream and moved toward the men.

Zol's heart hammered against his chest. He and Tungo moved closer. They crouched in a patch of berry bushes and held their breath. The hunters remained perfectly still so the mammoth would not trumpet an alarm to the herd.

The mammoth continued chewing on the grasses in her mouth. Zol and Tungo were close enough to hear the crunching, grinding noise of her giant teeth.

Then the hunters began to move again. Slowly they circled around behind the animal, keeping out of her sight. The boys sensed that something was about to happen soon.

Tungo whispered loudly to Zol, "Where's Nuba? I can't see my brother!"

Zol clamped his hand over Tungo's mouth and glared fiercely at him. Did he not remember their instructions? But Tungo yanked Zol's hand away and whispered, "I want to see him make the first jab!" He motioned to another patch of bushes closer to the hunters. "I'm going over there."

Zol frantically grabbed Tungo's arm and shook his head. No! But Tungo yanked himself free and ran out of the bushes, crouching low to the ground.

Even with its poor eyesight, the mammoth immediately noticed Tungo's movements. She stopped chewing to watch this strange creature running close to the ground. She raised her trunk to smell him. Then she started toward him.

Tungo was so intent on reaching the bushes that he did not see the mammoth moving toward him. Zol wanted to shout a warning, but he was afraid to disobey Yakono.

Zol watched in horror as the mammoth suddenly lowered her head and charged at Tungo. She caught him in her tusks and tossed him into the air like a piece of hide. Tungo flew through the air and landed in a limp heap near one of the mammoth's front feet.

"Tungo!" Zol screamed. If the mammoth stepped forward, she would crush Tungo like a fat frog, and his bloody body would be carried back to camp like Father's had so many seasons ago.

Zol looked to Tungo's brothers. Why did they just stand there? Had they been ordered to let Tungo be squashed under the mammoth's foot for disobeying? Why was Nuba not running under the mammoth now? Everything seemed to be frozen, like in one of his bad dreams.

Zol could not stand by and watch Tungo be trampled by the mammoth! Quickly, he nocked up his stone tooth in the spear-thrower and moved forward. He had only one stone tooth. He hoped his arm would remember how to adjust for its weight. Great Spirits!

He saw the mammoth raise her trunk and send a blaring scream back to the herd. Her neck was exposed. Now! Zol ran forward and threw the stone tooth with all his strength. The sharp spear hit true and sliced deep.

The mammoth's scream turned to a gurgle. Bright red blood spurted out the sides of her mouth. She staggered back and fell to her knees. Immediately, the rest of the hunters closed in with their spear-throwers, hurling spears from all sides.

Zol ran forward and dragged Tungo's limp body away. Tungo opened his eyes. "What happened?" he asked groggily. But Zol had no time to answer. The ground rumbled, telling the hunters that the mammoth's cries had summoned the rest of the herd.

Yakono motioned for the hunters to run for whatever cover they could find at the ice wall. Zol tried to run, but he was dragging Tungo, who still did not know what was happening.

Out of nowhere, Tungo's oldest brother swooped down and scooped up Tungo under one arm. With the other, he grabbed Zol's arm and ran for the protection of a small group of willow trees. There they hunkered down and tried to hide. The ground shook and the air filled with the bellowing cries of the approaching herd. Thick dust stirred up by the mammoth's feet made the boys cough, but it also helped to hide them.

Tungo's brother kept a protective arm on each boy as they crouched in the willow thicket. He would not let them move or speak while they watched the mammoths poke and prod their fallen member gently with sensitive trunks.

The mammoths grunted and trumpeted to the dead animal, trying to arouse her. Zol could not help feeling sorry for them. The animals obviously felt deeply the loss of one of their own.

A small mammoth left the herd and moved toward the willow thicket. Zol saw she had a big notch in her ear. It was *his* mammoth—the one that had touched him! She raised her trunk and scented the trees. She moved closer.

The herd, apparently satisfied that they could not help their fallen member, bellowed anguished cries and began to move away. The young mammoth with the torn ear turned to follow. The hunters breathed a sigh of relief. Zol suddenly realized that every muscle in his body was tensed.

That was why he almost jumped out of his skin when a strong hand grabbed his shoulder and yanked him up. Zol looked into the wide, angry face of their leader. Yakono's eyes crackled with anger, but his voice betrayed no emotion when he commanded, "Run and get the dogs—now!"

CHAPTER 36

KOOT'S GOODBYE

Only too happy to get away from there, Zol started running hard and fast. Thoughts raced through his mind as his feet pounded the ground: What would they do to Tungo while he was gone? What would happen to Zol when he returned? In his fear for Tungo's life, Zol had disobeyed their leader—unthinkable for a Star Dancer! What would Father have done?

For once, the act of running gave Zol no pleasure. He found the old men and the dogs where they had been told to wait. *They* had not disobeyed orders. The old hunters and the dogs took off immediately for the kill site, but Zol had to rest before starting back.

He lay on the grass to catch his breath and stared miserably into the endless sky. He saw a cloud of black dots circling and hovering over the kill site. Already alerted to the kill, crows and ravens would be feasting tonight.

The familiar ache of loss for Koot welled up inside and spilled out of Zol's eyes. Tears ran uncontrollably over his ears onto the ground. More than anything, right now, Zol wanted to look into that friendly black face and tell Koot what had happened today. He wanted to hear the crow's answering clucks and coos and to feel the bird push against his cheek.

As he watched the sky, Zol saw a small group of crows separate from the mass and head in his direction. Zol sat up and stared. Could it be? His heart skipped a beat when he saw one crow break away from the rest and fly toward him. He rubbed his eyes to make sure he was not dreaming. No, it was still there!

Zol jumped up and started running toward the crow. "Caw! Caw! Hellooo, Koot!" He called into the sky. "Hellooo, Koot! Hellooo, Koot!" He was practically screaming now.

He stopped and looked up, his heart beating hard. The crow now circled high over Zol's head. With both hands shielding his eyes against the brightness, Zol strained to watch the crow circle again and again, tighter and lower. Zol cupped his hands around his mouth and called again, "Caw! Hellooo, Koot!"

The crow spiraled out of the sky, ending in a side-slip, to land lightly on the ground in front of Zol. It cocked its head to one side and looked at Zol.

"Hello, Koot!" said Zol. He *must* be dreaming!

"Awwlo-koot," answered the crow. Then, in one graceful leap, the shiny black bird was on Zol's shoulder.

Zol could not believe this was happening. "Koot! It really is you, and you're alive!" Koot gripped Zol's shoulder with his strong claws and nibbled at the boy's ear, gurgling and cooing—obviously glad to see him, too.

Zol laughed. He felt like his heart would burst out of his chest. "Oh, Koot, I missed you so much!" He hugged the bird to him. "You're really alright, aren't you?" Zol ran his hand lovingly over the sun-drenched feathers and brought Koot down to his wrist, where he could look at his face.

"I've been so worried about you, Koot," said Zol. But you did it—you joined your own kind and survived! I'm proud of you."

Koot cocked his head almost upside down in that comical way of his, as if trying to understand Zol's words. "Koot-kom," he said and hopped back onto Zol's shoulder.

"Yes, you did," said Zol. Love for his crow flooded through him, and he shook his head in amazement. "How did you *know* that I needed to see you again?"

Suddenly Zol remembered his situation. "Koot, come. I have something important to show you." He started running and Koot flew along with him. The familiar "whoosh" of Koot's wings beating overhead was music to Zol's ears.

When they got to the kill site, it looked like an anthill. Hunters crawled all over the mammoth carcass and cut out great chunks of meat to be carried back to camp. One whole leg had been set aside for the dogs, who were tugging and tearing at it in a frenzy. They snapped and growled at each other as they fought for portions of the meat.

Relief flooded through Zol like melting ice when he saw Tungo perched on top of the dead mammoth's head. The hairy knob on top of the mammoth's head had been peeled back, and Tungo's arms were bloody up to his elbows. Zol realized that Tungo's punishment had begun: To him had fallen the hateful job of scooping out the brains. Tungo was stuffing the slippery brains into a bladder bag to carry back to camp so they could be used later for tanning the hide. Zol knew how humiliated he must be. But at least he was alive!

"Look, Koot," said Zol, running his hand over the bird on his shoulder and pointing to the carcass. "I did it, too. I helped kill it, Koot, and I wasn't afraid." He brought the crow around to face him. "I think my father sent me courage through his spear-thrower, Koot. Did you fly to him and give him my message?"

Koot hopped to Zol's head and began preening the boy's hair with his beak like he used to. The other crows circled and screeched overhead, waiting their turn at the carcass. Suddenly Koot dropped back to Zol's shoulder and stiffened, staring up at the flock.

"What is it, my friend?" asked Zol, rubbing his cheek against the shiny feathers. But Koot did not give an answering push against Zol like he usually did. Instead, Zol felt the familiar digging in of Koot's claws as they pushed off from his shoulder.

Zol watched the black form rise into the air and heard Koot's answering call to the flock. Something in Koot's call made Zol's heart sink. He knew it would be the last time he would see his crow. This visit had been a gift. His throat tightened.

"Good-bye, Koot," he called after the bird. "Good-bye, my friend. I'll never forget you!" The painful knot in the back of his throat made it hard to swallow. Sunlight glinted off the blue-black wings as they pushed against the air. "Koot!" he yelled after the crow. "Tell my father! Tell him I wasn't afraid, Koot!"

Zol stood still, watching Koot make circles over him in the incredibly blue sky. "Caw! Caw!" he called.

"Caw! Caw!" came the answering call. The crow circled again and again, as if reluctant to leave.

Then Zol watched Koot fly toward the flock and become just one of the black dots. "We did it, Koot," said Zol softly. "We both did it."

The ache in Zol's throat was unbearable. But he would not cry. This was the way things had to be, and Zol knew it. Somehow he did not feel like a boy anymore. He would be a brave hunter; he knew that now. Father could be proud of him.

Someday, around a campfire, Zol knew he would tell the story of Koot, the crow who could talk. He would tell how he, Zol, had been able to call him out of the sky. But right now he had something more important to do. He had to find Yakono and take his punishment like a Star Dancer. His fears would not control him anymore.

Zol turned and ran toward the mammoth.

GLOSSARY

Balsamroot: Plant with large, arrow-shaped leaves and yellow flowers; parts of plant used by prehistoric people for food.

Burn slab*: Broad, flat granite stone used by Star Dancers in burning ceremony to send spirits of dead to the sky.

Camas: Spiky, blue flower common in mountain meadows of Pacific Northwest; the bulb was a nutritious food source for prehistoric people.

Carnelian: Type of clear stone, reddish-brown in color.

Chert: A type of rock commonly used to make stone points.

Chokecherry: A type of tree.

Dart: Stone point hafted to short shaft, ready to fit into longer shaft for launching with spear-thrower.

Flintknapper: One who makes points and tools from rocks.

Hafted: Stone spear point fitted to wooden shaft and bound with strips of sinew.

Ho!*: A greeting.

Hoopa!*: Exclamation of delight.

Hotu*: Shelter made of poles covered with hide; similar to Indian tipi.

Knap: To break or split rocks into flakes, which can then be shaped into spear points, hide scrapers, and other tools of the stone age.

Moccasins: Soft slippers made from animal hides.

Mullein: Plant used for food and medicine; dried stalks also made into torches.

Nocked: A spear hooked into a spear-thrower, ready to thrust.

Obsidian: A glassy, volcanic material used to make spear points and tools; usually black.

Ochre: A soft mineral found in nature (usually red or yellow); crushed and used as paint by prehistoric people.

Owk!*: Exclamation of pain or surprise.

Oya*: Expression of agreement; okay, sure.

Pemmican: "Sausage" of dried meat, mixed with dried berries and animal fat (and sometimes ground nuts). Mixture was packed into cleaned animal intestines and stored for winter use.

Preening: What birds do with their beaks to clean and smooth their feathers.

Root cake: Flat cakes made from cooked roots or bulbs, then dried; sometimes included nuts or berries.

Sinew: Tough cording made from animal tendons; used for sewing and binding.

Sledge: A platform on pole runners; pulled by dogs to carry loads across rough ground.

Steppe: A large expanse of grass-covered plains; grasslands.

Tuber: Thick underground stem of a plant, like a potato.

* Fictional words made up by the author.

Photo by Stan Bryant

Patricia Nikolina Clark lives in Washington State with her husband, their energetic dog, and a cat named Stump.

Her passion for prehistory leads her to volunteer in archaeological excavations whenever possible. The idea for this book came during her participation in a dig that uncovered a cache of stone points dated to the Clovis period. She held in her hands a stone point once held by a Clovis hunter— 12,000 years ago! It was then that Zol tapped her on her shoulder and began whispering his story in her ear.

Patricia's stories and articles have appeared in children's magazines for many years Her easy-reader, *Goodbye, Goose,* was published in 2000. This is her first novel for children.